CLEAR
CONFUSION

CLEAR
CONFUSION

KATHY M. HOWARD

AMBASSADOR INTERNATIONAL
GREENVILLE, SOUTH CAROLINA & BELFAST, NORTHERN IRELAND

www.ambassador-international.com

Clear Confusion

© 2019 by Kathy M. Howard
All rights reserved

ISBN: 978-1-62020-902-8
eISBN: 978-1-62020-914-1

No part of this publication may be reproduced, distributed, or transmitted in any form or by any means, including photocopying, recording, or other electronic or mechanical methods, without the prior written permission of the publisher, except in the case of brief quotations embodied in critical reviews and certain other non-commercial uses permitted by copyright law. For permission requests, contact the publisher using the information below.

This is a work of fiction. Names, characters, and incidents are all products of the author's imagination or are used for fictional purposes. Any resemblance to actual events or persons, living or dead, is entirely coincidental. Any mentioned brand names, places, and trademarks remain the property of their respective owners, bear no association with the author or the publisher, and are used for fictional purposes only.

Scripture taken from the The Ryrie Study Bible: New International Version Copyright © 1973, 1978, 1984 International Bible Society. Used by permission of Zondervan Bible Publishers.

Cover Design & Typesetting by Hannah Nichols
Ebook Conversion by Anna Riebe Raats
Edited by Katie Cruice Smith

Author Photo by Sharon Brisken

AMBASSADOR INTERNATIONAL
Emerald House
411 University Ridge, Suite B14
Greenville, SC 29601, USA
www.ambassador-international.com

AMBASSADOR BOOKS
The Mount
2 Woodstock Link
Belfast, BT6 8DD, Northern Ireland, UK
www.ambassadormedia.co.uk

The colophon is a trademark of Ambassador, a Christian publishing company.

DEDICATION

To God ~ always and forever!

To my first cousins: Matt, Todd, Ashley, Sheena, Will, Rebecca, Leigh, Angie, Tonya, Chris, Joel, Nicole, Jenn, Julia, Jared, Jessica, and Jenna ~ thanks for the childhood memories.

To my adulthood hometown of Blackshear, Georgia ~ thanks for all the love and support and for the inspiration. I never knew small town life, pine trees, and hunting could feel so much like home.

ACKNOWLEDGMENT

Mom, anyone who puts as much time as you do talking out scenes, editing, and encouraging deserves her name in lights and a Snicker bar the size of Texas. I love you!

When I am afraid, I will trust in you.

—Psalm 56:3

CHAPTER ONE

Thursday, April 7

1:15 a.m.

"C'mon man! We gotta get to her before she squeals!"

Charlotte froze, too scared to move. They were frightfully close. She heard the shorter man's jittery energy penetrate his country voice.

"I bet she's headed out the side, through the grocery section. Go that way," he ordered. "I'll head up front. Make sure nothin's outta the ordinary, and she ain't hit up nobody for help."

Charlotte bit her bottom lip. This wasn't going to end well if they split up. Or would it?

"All right, but stay calm. Lay low. What happened was bad enough. Let's not make it worse." He let out an exasperated breath. "If you don't find her in a few minutes or you get the notion she's talked, forget her. Just get out of here as fast as you can and meet back at the rendezvous point. We can always deal with the girl later." The man kept his voice just above a whisper, unlike his partner who seemed ready to explode. "She didn't see us; I'd bet my life on it. She was too scared to stick around and look closely." *But that didn't mean he hadn't gotten a good, clear look at her.*

"She better not have!" Adrenaline and nervous anger echoed in his words. "Roland'll know what to do. He took care of things last time

9

someone snooped, and I ain't seen that one since. This one won't be no different. She ain't gonna get far—not if she's alone."

"Agreed." The voices drifted as the men began searching for Charlotte, and she frantically searched for protection. The fact that it was just after one a.m. didn't help. She was already too tired to function properly, much less form a coherent thought. And now her life depended on her ability to strategically devise an escape plan. *Oh, why didn't I bring my phone? Help me, God. Please!*

The large superstore, open twenty-four hours a day, used every inch of the building to showcase its merchandise. Bins full of items overcrowded each aisle, causing chaos for the shopper in search of something in particular. Charlotte thought she could use that to her advantage. The toy and furniture divisions overlapped, eliminating potentially open sections. A giant, overstuffed panda in the toy department could make a good hiding place if she squeezed between it and the stack of beanbag chairs against the wall.

She carefully peeked around the aisle where she'd stood frozen into the area of slim traffic. Very few people were in the store, and all completely unaware of what'd just happened. She had to somehow get to the panda without being seen by her trackers or the general public. If a bystander caught sight of someone hiding among the toys, he'd likely point and bring attention to her. She couldn't afford to be seen by anyone for fear of someone else getting hurt. The two men seemed careless. One wrong move, no matter the intent, could cause a dangerous reaction. No, she'd have to stay hidden until the men were completely gone; then she could find the proper authorities. Surely, they'd give up looking for her sooner rather than later. It wouldn't be long before the body was found.

5:30 a.m.

The woman awoke to the sound of wind dancing rather loudly through the treetops and a strange sense of fear. Underneath her, a cool, hard ground gave off a scent of wet mud, causing her nostrils to crinkle.

Inside, her head pounded with her heartbeat. She squeezed her eyes shut, giving herself a minute. It didn't do much good. Her mind was too fuzzy to successfully decipher her bearings. Somehow an internal fog blocked her ability to reason.

God, where am I?

Although she heard evidence of early morning hours, it was dark, practically pitch black. Nothing visible beyond a few feet, and even that was blurry. Another gust of wind blew, bringing a breeze across her left cheek. A few goose bumps appeared. The other side of her face, shielded from the gust, remained impressed in dried mud. Although it was hard, it felt icky pasted against her skin. She tried to gently pull herself out of the crusted grime but found the movement harder than she'd expected.

The muscles in her arms and legs were sore—really sore. But why? She sat up tenderly, placing a hand on her forehead. The effort to lift her body proved difficult. Carefully and ever so slowly, she stood the rest of the way. With one hand steadying her head and the other out-stretched, she inched her feet forward, searching for something sturdy.

Why do I have on only one shoe? Where is my other shoe?

A large oak tree stood about ten feet away. It was rough to the touch, but strong. She placed her searching hand on the solid trunk, lowered herself back to the hard ground, and rested her back and aching head against the tree. Darkness and pain—she wasn't going anywhere anytime soon.

Her stomach growled, begging for sustenance. Food might help her headache—if she had any. She patted her pockets, hoping. Nothing. For the life of her, she couldn't figure out exactly where she was or how she'd gotten there or why she'd be in such an area. The only thing she could do was focus on what she did know. It was dark. She couldn't see anything, though she felt sure she was somewhere in the woods. Mosquitoes buzzed in her ear, threatening to bite her. And aside from a headache, she was also hungry and ridiculously sore.

Without a clear visual of her surroundings, she knew she shouldn't move far. What if she stumbled down a cliff or into a pond? She was better off just trying to go back to sleep until daylight. Next to an aspirin, sleep was the best thing.

With no other options, the woman closed her eyes. She breathed in the darkness and eventually began to drift. Sleep came easier than she'd thought possible, given her situation and surroundings.

As she slept, she dreamt in flashes crammed with feelings of utter confusion. The dreams were harsh and unclear. Blackness, followed quickly by an intense strobe of light, and then black again filled her subconscious. It felt like she was sitting in a cave, staring into nothing, as a light suddenly and rapidly turned on and off, making it impossible for her eyes to focus. The pattern of dark to light quickened, intensifying so much that she physically felt it behind her eyes. She jerked herself awake. The headache was worse.

Her eyes blinked repeatedly as a glaring, bright light shone directly at her. She saw nothing but white.

"Hello?"

The baritone voice surprised her, releasing an unexplained fear throughout her body. The woman lifted a sore arm in an effort to shield the light and locate its origin. The light lowered, but remained on. It took a few seconds for her eyes to adjust. Once they did, she glimpsed a blurry vision of brown boots and a lot of green. The voice's owner squatted, placing the flashlight on the ground. Her focus zeroed in on a somewhat grizzly, brown-haired man, crouched next to her and holding a shotgun in his right hand. A shiver ran through her at the sight of the weapon. She quickly jumped up, stepping backwards. The movement brought her immediate pain.

It hurts to move. Please don't let him shoot me, God! Please!

"Ma'am?"

"Go away!" She croaked.

The man stood and stepped forward, inching toward her. He extended his hand in an effort to close the distance, but she leaned away from his reach. Could she make a run for it? It was still too dark to see anything past the flashlight. But did that really matter? She could at least try, couldn't she?

"I wouldn't if I were you."

"What?" Her voice cracked. Was he threatening her? She hesitated only a second before she turned and ran as fast as she could into the darkness. All she could do was keep her arms extended in hopes of avoiding trees and branches.

After several yards, her ankle turned when her shoeless foot stepped into a shallow hole, bringing her to the ground.

"Ah!" she whimpered, biting her lip.

Now she was stuck. She had no escape, nowhere to go. The man was close. She could hear his breathing. She blinked back a tear of fear and pain.

"Help! Help!" Vomit rose to her throat. Nausea came with it.

The man stopped. "Whoa, now. What's with the hollering? I'm not going to hurt you."

"Help! Somebody help me!"

"Lady, I promise. I'm *not* going to hurt you." He backed up. "I just wanted to see if you were lost—if you were okay. It's not everyday you run into someone sleeping in the woods. I'll leave you alone, if that's what you want."

She shivered and frowned, holding her tender ankle. Lost, confused, hungry, exhausted, and in pain. She didn't have much of a choice. She would have to trust him. He would help her, or he would hurt her. Either way, the misery would disappear by his hands.

Gingerly, she opened her eyes and whispered, "You . . . have a gun."

"Yeah, my friend and I are headed over there to hunt." It looked like he pointed to the right of her, but she could barely see the gesture. "We were trying to get there before daylight to surprise the turkeys. However, after all that yelling, I don't believe we'll be much of a surprise."

"Hunting?"

"Yes. Just hunting." The man laid the gun down and took a step closer, shining the flashlight on himself, so she could get a better look. He was covered in camouflage from head to toe.

She released a heavy sigh. "Oh. Sorry."

"It's okay." He took the flashlight off of himself and shone it on the woman. She shivered again. Mud covered her face, making it hard to see her features. A streak ran down her cheek, indicating she had been crying. There was dried blood in her hair, and she held her hands around her ankle, grimacing. She looked to be frightened and in a good bit of pain. She needed help.

"Ma'am? May I come closer?"he asked. She barely nodded. He walked to her, bending down close enough to get a glimpse of her eyes. They were dark. "I'd like to shine my light into your eyes to check for a concussion. Would that be okay?"

Again, she nodded slowly. He pulled the flashlight up and looked closely into her eyes. She winced immediately. He wasn't going to be able to test his presumption. It was obvious the brightness hurt her. So he lowered the flashlight to her left ankle instead, where her hand rested.

"May I?"

She removed her hand. He couldn't see any immediate swelling or discoloration.

"This may need some ice, but I think it's okay. Are you alone?"

Was she alone? She really didn't know. She couldn't think. Nothing made sense.

"My head. My ankle. It all hurts," she answered instead. Her voice was weak.

The man looked over his shoulder and called, "Hey, Vin. Come here and help me." Another hunter emerged from the darkness and stood beside his friend. "Okay, ma'am. I really think we need to get you back to town. The doctor there is a good man; and quite frankly, I'd feel better if he took a look at you. You mind if I carry you to my truck and then drive you into town? My good friend Vincent here will come with us. I promise, we're not going to harm you. We just want to help."

The woman turned to look at Vincent. He was dressed in camouflage as well. He looked at her, studying her intently. She nodded a final time, knowing there wasn't another option.

The first hunter placed his arms underneath her knees and around her back. He stood carefully, trying to prevent the sway of her legs.

Vincent grabbed the guns and the flashlight, holding it out far enough to light the way.

Even though the man carried her gently and walked slowly, her legs swayed. He could hear the pain in her moans. Whatever was going on with her was too much. Before the three of them made it to the truck, the woman had passed out in the arms of the hunter.

6:45 a.m.

Nicholas changed his mind as soon as the woman went unconscious. He decided to call Dr. Mitchell on his way, instead of waiting in the parking lot until the office opened for an immediate appointment. He knew the man would already be at work. The doctor used the hour before their doors opened to patients at 7:30 to catch up on paperwork and to enjoy a cup of coffee in peace and quiet.

He tapped his thumb on the steering wheel, waiting for an answer or the automatic recording to kick in.

"Jennings Family Practice."

"Doc, I'm glad I got you." Nicholas exhaled. "It's Nicholas. We've got a bit of a situation. Vin and I found a young woman in the woods. Looks like she's been through the wringer—dirty, dried blood in her hair, missing shoe, pretty messed up ankle, and says her head hurts. She was coherent a few minutes ago—scared but talking. But now she's unconscious. I think she'll be all right, but I sure would feel better if you could check her out. Can you see her now at your office, or do I need to take her on to the hospital?"

"Who is she?"

"I don't know. We don't recognize her. Never got around to asking her name."

"How's her breathing?"

"Fine, I guess."

"Any other significant injuries?"

"Other than her ankle and maybe head? Not that I could tell."

Dr. Mitchell asked several questions, all of which Nicholas could not give a definitive answer, so he agreed to meet them at the hospital. He'd planned to see three other patients there later that day anyway. Going a few hours earlier than planned wouldn't hurt. His P.A. could see to his morning patients while he was away.

Good. At least there was a plan, and help was on its way. Nicholas didn't like the way they'd found the young woman. It did not sit well with him at all.

He peered at the lady in his truck. She lay across the back seat, almost lifeless in her form. Passed out and in the window's light of daybreak, she seemed fragile, and at the same time, quite strong. Her face didn't look as frightened as it had an hour ago, though she did look as if she'd been through an ordeal. Even with the mud on her face, Nicholas could tell she wasn't much older than thirty. What had happened to her? For a small town, she was an intriguing mystery waiting to be solved. She started to moan.

Nicholas pulled the car over.

"Vin, jump back there and try to keep her as still as possible. This jarring may make her pain worse."

"Uh," Vincent exhaled.

"Just do the best you can. Step on whatever you need to. I'm more worried about her than the gear."

"Uh, yeah, sure." Vincent grunted as he maneuvered into the backseat. A pop sounded. "There goes the decoy."

Vincent positioned his long legs the best he could amongst all the hunting gear as Nicholas drove off. Then he laid her legs across his lap, being careful with the left one, and leaned forward, ready to grab her shoulders if they hit a bumpy part of the road. No good would come from her falling off the seat.

"She's starting to move."

"That's good," said Nicholas. He'd sure like to talk to her again before they arrived at the hospital. "See if there's any more water in that cooler. She may want some when she wakes up."

Vincent reached into the miniature cooler by his feet and pulled out the last bottle of water. He stuck it in the door's cupholder and then turned to study the woman beside him. Her eyes fluttered. Her head turned slightly from side to side. He leaned in closer, trying to get a better look at the blood in her hair. There could be an ugly gash under that pretty blonde hair of hers. It was hard to tell. She was such a mess. Just as he reached to touch a bloody cluster of hair, her eyes suddenly flew open. Vincent startled. The woman's body bounced in response.

"Ooh!" she mouthed.

"Sss . . . sorry."

Slowly, she slid upright, keeping her legs extended.

"Hi," he said coolly, trying to regain his composure.

"She awake?" came from the driver's seat. Vincent only nodded.

"Hello," she responded in a faint voice, barely audible.

"You remember me?"

She winced slightly and squinted, trying to make out the individual addressing her. Vincent leaned closer. She eyed him carefully.

"The woods?" she asked cautiously.

"Yeah . . . the woods. My buddy . . . uh, Nick . . . and I carried you out. We're taking you to the hospital." He stared closely at her eyes. They were a dim brown and somewhat blank. She returned his intense gaze for a moment and then glanced out the window.

Nicholas risked a glance over his shoulder in high traffic and smiled.

"Well, hello there, young lady. How you feeling?"

She rubbed her eyes. "Okay, I guess. My head hurts like the dickens, though."

"Would you like something to drink?" Nicholas asked. "Vin's got some water for you."

She tried repositioning. It was a difficult move, especially with all the clutter and because the man beside her looked as helpless as she felt.

Once she was situated, Vincent opened the bottle and handed it to her.

"Thank you," she whispered.

She took a sip, sighed, and proceeded to gulp the rest. She'd not realized how thirsty she'd become. The man driving laughed. Now that she was sitting straighter, he had a clear sight of her through the rearview mirror.

"You want me to stop and get you another?"

"No, I think I'm good for now," she responded, forming an embarrassed smile. Vincent took the empty bottle from her extended hand and tossed it on the floorboard.

"Where's the hospital?"

Vincent chose to answer, watching her closely as he did. "A little ways. The closest hospital is thirty minutes from town. We've got another ten minutes or so."

The woman went stiff. "Oh." Anxiety crept in. Was her rescue just a ruse? How could a hospital be thirty minutes from civilization? Were they playing a game with her? She was in a moving vehicle, trapped just as badly as she'd been in the woods. Again, there was nowhere to escape.

Nicholas straightened his back, feeling it pop as he did. It was a habit he struggled to break. He noticed the woman's expression change. "You're not scared of us again, are you?"

His voice was calm. She diverted her eyes back out the window. Everything was blurry, each tree running into the other. Why couldn't she just relax?

"Maybe it would help to get to know each other. That way we're not all just strangers heading to a hospital," Nicholas encouraged. "I'm Nicholas Nelson. And the quiet one in the back there is my long-time friend, Vincent Cobb." He grinned. "Okay, now what's your name, little lady?"

She was so confused, surrounded by the two men. One minute, she feared them; and the next, she wasn't sure what she felt. Her mouth opened to answer. "I'm . . . I'm." She squinted her eyes in confusion. "I'm." She suddenly realized she didn't know who she was. "I'm sorry. I . . . I don't know. I don't know who I am." Her eyes widened. Panic rose. How could she not know who she was?

Nicholas started to speak and then hesitated. How were they to respond to that? The poor girl had obviously had an awfully rough night. He cleared his throat and whispered kindly, "I'm sure it'll come to you in no time."

She frowned. *Hopefully.*

11:00 a.m.

The young woman sat on the worn examining table wearing a pale blue, paper gown. She had cuts and bruises in places she hadn't realized. Thankfully, they didn't hurt. Her unreal situation had been so dominant in her mind, these simple wounds seemed superficial.

Without any memory of who she was or how she'd ended up in the woods, she'd hesitantly agreed when Dr. Mitchell and the ER doctor on call had insisted on a full examination, a CT scan, and multiple interactions with other hospital personnel, including a social worker. All were very kind, except for the town doctor. His bedside manners left a lot to be desired.

She watched the aging man's face as he scrawled his conclusions in an open folder, narrowing his eyes in concentration. He wasn't very talkative. He came across as detached and uncaring. He asked questions without emotion or tenderness. How could someone take care of others for a living and yet seem not to actually care *about* them?

Dr. Mitchell put down the pen and swiveled his metal stool around to face his patient. He sighed. "You have a relatively deep laceration on the side of your head that should heal without complication. The stitches we put in will dissolve within a week or two. The rest of your scratches can be treated with antiseptic and bandages. Your ankle will be fine in a couple of days. Don't put any weight on it for the rest of the day. We'll give you some crutches to help and wrap the ankle before you leave. Keep it elevated two to three hours today and tomorrow, and ice it for about fifteen minutes every couple of hours this afternoon. If there was any swelling, it has already gone down, which is a good sign. The ice is more a precaution. In my opinion, its pain was brought on more by your exhaustion than actual injury."

He pulled off his glasses, laying them on the counter. "The main issue, of course, is a concussion. That seems to be what is causing your memory loss. You will need to take it slow and easy for the next several days. And for the next twenty-four hours, someone will need to be with you at all times, closely monitoring you."

He cleared his throat as he began clicking the pen opened and closed. "Are you sure you do not have any recollection of a family member or friend, even a hint of someone? Is there a city or school that possibly rings a bell?"

She pulled her lower lip under her teeth, desperate for a glimmer of recollection. "No, nothing at all. Nothing comes to mind," she answered, blinking back a burning tear. "My memory *will* return, though, won't it, Doctor?"

He scratched the back of his head and responded indifferently. "It should."

She waited for him to say more, to explain, to go into a detailed reason behind the short answer. When he didn't, she shook her head in disbelief and repeated his comment. "It should?"

She hadn't lingered too long on the possibility that her not knowing who she was would last more than a day. Now however, after hearing the unsympathetic doctor's hollow prediction, she could think of nothing else. Again, just like in the truck, panic overcame her. Her breaths quickened simultaneously with her rising heartbeat thumping in her neck.

"What does that mean—it *should*? You mean it might *not*?"

"Time usually tells in this sort of thing. There's nothing else wrong with you, except the aforementioned minor injuries. Your CT scan was rushed to the radiologist for reading, and it came back clean—no bleeding on the brain." He spoke every sentence at the same pitch; no word was emphasized over another. "But because of the concussion, don't do anything strenuous or for long periods at a time, even reading, for the next couple of days. After that, introduce activity slowly and carefully until you've been given my all-clear."

"But?" Her head started to hurt again. The doctor almost looked annoyed that she wasn't taking the news with ease. He apparently did not like to be bothered with questions. "But what do I do? I have no money. Where do I go? I don't even know where I was when they found me!"

His expression didn't change. It was like his face was carved out of stone, with no sympathy as he answered matter-of-factly, "You were found in Jennings, a small town in south Georgia. As for what you should do—rules are somewhat sketchy in these parts concerning a non-threatening, otherwise-healthy adult with amnesia. As long as you agree to stick around until I clear you, the social worker will likely question you again, make the proper authorities aware of the situation, and set you up with someone in town to watch over you. That is, if you refuse to stay overnight at the hospital for observation."

A fear greater than the thought of her memory not returning embraced her. She could not explain it, but the idea of being watched over and observed unnerved her.

"If I don't stay at the hospital, would I be set up with someone like a nurse or police officer?"

He grunted, seemingly bothered. "Yes, probably, but not necessarily. Like I said, Jennings is a small town. Everyone knows everyone. As long as the person is trustworthy, the social worker will likely make allowances. If you're uncomfortable with the idea of another stranger filling that job, I suggest you speak with Nicholas Nelson, the man who brought you in. He does a lot of odd jobs around the county. He may know of a place for you to stay that would satisfy you."

Dr. Mitchell shut her folder and dabbed a tissue to his watery eye. Allergies. "Your blurry vision, I believe, is not a result of your head injury. Nicholas went back to the woods after he dropped you off and found these not far from where he found you. If I'm right, they are yours."

He handed her a pair of dark, wire-framed glasses. She tried them on, and everything became suddenly clear. A sigh of relief escaped. At least one problem was solved.

The doctor cleared his throat, satisfied in his prediction. "Because the rules in this situation are not technically law-breaking ones, I would strongly suggest you still abide by my and the social worker's suggestions. You should stay in town for a while, definitely until I clear you and hopefully until your memory returns or a loved one is located."

He looked at the woman, her eyes glazing over. She was obviously distraught, almost on the verge of hysterics, if he had to guess. His job was to stitch her up and give her something for her headache. He was not a social worker or a counselor. He was a doctor. He'd never been good at anything else. He treated ailments, not emotions.

"Now," he continued. "I'd like to see you again in a few days, to re-examine your head and ankle."

She looked at the professional in front of her, dumbfounded. He'd reopened her file and was already busy scribbling his final notes, obviously ready to dismiss her.

What am I going to do, God? Who am I?

She felt lost, physically and mentally, with no idea of who she was. She didn't even know what kind of a person she was. Was she a hardworking woman who loved the spotlight and the outdoors, or was she a quiet introvert? Was she kind, or was she someone no one wanted to be around? She could be anyone. There were so many open-ended questions. It was as if she'd stepped into someone else's mind, someone who thought of nothing, someone living in a cave with no entrance or exit. The mind was completely empty except for the last few hours and, thankfully, her knowledge of God. *If I'd forgotten Him, too!* She shuttered at the thought.

She looked curiously at the physician, trying desperately to pull in a realistic thought. He wasn't going to offer any help, not the kind she really needed. The only direction he'd given her was professional information and a suggestion to talk to the man who'd found her in the woods. She didn't have much of a choice. The idea of staying in the hospital did not seem desirable for some reason. So, she'd speak with the social worker, agree to stay for the time being, and strongly consider seeking out help from the hunter. Nicholas Nelson, at least, seemed friendlier than the so-called expert.

Nicholas lowered his head and rubbed the back of his neck. What had he just agreed to take on? He'd spent the last twenty-five minutes talking to Roberta Perry, one of the hospital's social workers. Roberta was a local—born and raised in Jennings—and graduated high school a couple of years ahead of Nicholas. Their families knew each other well. He answered all her questions; and before he knew it, he'd volunteered his services, or rather, his sister's. Roberta agreed, but only after she'd spoken with Dr. Mitchell's patient.

"Sorry for screaming earlier—in the woods."

Nicholas lifted his head, seeing the young woman and Roberta making their way over to them. He smiled and stood. "That surely doesn't need apologizing for. I've got a younger sister. I have always told her to yell as loud as she could if she ever felt she was in danger. You were only doing what comes natural and what you should've done."

She grinned, still embarrassed.

"I see you have a new ride," he joked, pointing to the crutches. "Looks like you're already a pro."

"Thanks . . . Nicholas, is it?"

"Yes, ma'am, that's me. Most people call me Nick, but I prefer Nicholas. My dad is Nick, and it causes a lot of confusion when you don't know which Nick people are talking about."

She grinned. He was definitely friendlier than the doctor. She faced his companion. "And Vincent?"

"Uh, yes. Vincent Cobb."

"And do people call you something different?"

He looked caught off-guard for some reason. "Nick calls me Vin, but everyone else pretty much sticks with Vincent." The smile he wore seemed forced, intentional. He was a bit pale, and his tall, lanky body wobbled.

She looked at him curiously. "Are you okay?"

Nicholas started laughing, slapping his friend on the back. "Vin here's not the biggest fan of hospitals. I'm impressed he's made it here as long as he has."

"Oh, I see."

"You all finished?" Nicholas asked Roberta, still grinning.

"We are." Roberta turned to the woman and handed her something. "Now, if you have any questions or concerns, here's my card.

Call anytime. Otherwise, I'll be checking in often until this is resolved. Remember to follow Dr. Mitchell's orders."

The woman nodded. "Thank you."

Although the social worker had been considerably more empathetic than the doctor, she still hadn't done anything to ease the woman's mind. She felt like she was just being passed from one person to the next, and it rattled her.

She subconsciously reached up, searching for the stitches, as they said their goodbyes. The skin was still numb from the Novocaine shot, but she could feel the uncomfortable pull of the sutures.

"Nicholas, thank you. Dr. Mitchell said you went back and found my glasses."

"No problem. Glad to see the squinting has stopped," he winked.

Vincent tightened his jaw as he looked at his watch. "I need to go."

"Half a day's work is better than none." Nicholas held the door opened as they stepped into the morning light. "Let me drop Vin off at his house, so he can get to work, and we'll head on over to my sister's. Her place is down the street from Vin's. Then you can get cleaned up."

The tired woman breathed a short sigh of relief. "Cleaned up" meant a shower. A change of clothes. This man was already offering the help she needed.

"That sounds wonderful. Thank you."

The three of them piled into Nicholas' four-door, gray F-150 Ford truck, allowing the woman to sit in the front passenger seat next to Nicholas. The truck was fully loaded with burgundy leather seats, a sunroof, and XM radio. For such a beautiful vehicle, it was quite messy. There were camouflage duffel bags and extra hunting clothes, including a couple of turkey vests, scattered across the floor of the backseat.

Vincent looked uncomfortable as he tried to position himself between all the gear and added crutches. Two shotguns sat on his left side, sending uneasiness through the woman. For some reason, she felt the sport of hunting did not sit well with her. She shivered.

Nicholas leaned forward, pressing a button on the control panels. Within a few seconds, she felt warmth eluding from her seat. Seat warmers. He'd misinterpreted her shiver. She closed her eyes and let the heat travel throughout her body. It felt good, soothing. They sat in silence for a couple of minutes, riding through town, each reliving the early morning hours. The sun had long since risen, clearing away any remnants of the night and bringing with it the start of day—a day already in deep motion.

"Did you happen to remember anything while you were with the doctor? Your name or where you came from?" asked Vincent, breaking the silence with the question both men were thinking.

Opening her eyes, she responded faintly, "No, nothing. I have no idea who I am, how old I am, where I came from, or anything." Understandable sadness tainted her voice. Her thoughts were such a jumbled mess, she couldn't figure out how to disentangle them. She felt like her mind was a ball of yarn with the end tucked deep inside, just far enough away from her unraveling reach.

"I've thought about a family, of friends, and co-workers. Anyone missing me? Is there a husband or a child out there without a wife or mother? Parents? Grandparents? I've thought about a reason for being in the woods. Was I with someone, and somehow, we got separated? What if there's someone else still out there? Why was I there? Where was I going, and where was I coming from?" She spoke quickly as the questions came to her one after another.

The men heard a deep sigh. "It's just so much to take in, to grasp. I'm trying hard not to let any of that scare me, but I don't think I'm doing a very good job of it."

The confused woman let out her thoughts, choosing to express her concerns and fears to perfect strangers. Vincent knew Nicholas was pondering what she said as much as he was. His friend was the type to fix what he could. He'd find more time today to comb through those woods again, to make sure no one else was there. He'd do it himself, even though the authorities were there now. But he'd do it without making a big deal of it. He'd already spoken to his friend, a deputy for the Jennings Police Department, as Dr. Mitchell examined the girl. No one had yet reported anyone missing matching her description.

Vincent silently thought through all her questions. They were most of his as well. He'd have to wait to find the answers when she did. He wasn't sure what else to say.

"Sorry." He sat, staring at the back of the passenger seat. She was shorter than the seat, so all he saw were a few strands of hair escaping underneath the headrest.

Nicholas suddenly slapped the steering wheel, sending the woman jumping. "Oops, I keep doing that, don't I?" he said apologetically. He gave her a second to calm down. "I've got an idea. Why don't we come up with a name that you can go by until your memory does come back? Might be fun, you know, getting to pick your own name. Whaddaya say?"

She grimaced, trying hard to see the fun in her situation. It wasn't fun. It was frightening and unnerving. Still, she would need to go by something. She'd need a name of some kind. Otherwise, she'd have to answer indefinitely to "hey, you" or "lady."

"Okay." She leaned up and pressed the button, turning off her seat warmer. It was getting hot, thinking about her unknown future. "Any suggestions?"

An overly enthusiastic smile pulled at the corners of Nicholas' lips. "Plenty. How about Virginia or Chloe or Ella?" he asked, tapping his finger on his chin in a feigned expression of thoughtfulness. "Or, um, let's see . . . there's Claire or Clara . . . Franny?" She grunted. "No," he shook his head in response, "not Franny—too childish sounding."

"Karen?" came from the back seat. Nicholas laughed, peering at his friend through the rearview mirror.

"Your ex? Really, man?"

"Nope, guess not. It was the only name I could think of." He lowered his head, studying his boots.

The woman rolled her eyes in frustration. None of those names sounded right.

"Okay, um . . . " Nicholas thought. "Let's see. There's Victoria, or Sydney, or Rachel. Or if you think you might like a more traditional name, there's Mary, or Sara, or Elizabeth. Then there are your really uncommon ones like Odessa or Veruca. Veruca might be a fun name." She crinkled her nose at the last two suggestions. "Any of those sound appealing?"

She thought carefully about what it would feel to be called by one of those names. None of them rang a bell or felt like home, but she'd need to choose one. She needed an identity, even if it was only temporary.

"Sydney. I guess Sydney will do."

He smiled widely. "Sydney it is. It's nice to meet you, Sydney."

1:30 p.m.

Now that she could see without squinting, Sydney peered out the window of the truck as they drove through town, heading to Vincent's house. The day was bright and sunny. Wind gently blew through the trees, sending a mixed message of contentment. She frowned slightly, feeling that if she weren't in this predicament, she'd probably enjoy being outside in this weather. Something pulled at her to roll down the window and let the breeze and warmth of the sun's rays slide over her skin. It felt like an electric charge running through her, from the top of her head to the tips of her toes, giving her an ounce of much-needed energy. She laid her head on her propped arm, halfway out of the vehicle, trying to keep the current flowing.

Traffic was light. There were four red lights spread throughout the town with several stores lining each side of Main Street. A few of the stores were local shops, selling clothing or yogurt and home-made goodies or other paraphernalia. A hardware store and two drug stores sat across the street from each other. Consignment shops and discount stores of everyday essentials looked to be the most common, with one at almost every intersection. A family-owned grocery store stood at the heart of the town, across from the courthouse, which was beautiful. It was two stories, made entirely of brick. The design looked old, but the building looked new. A simple fountain stood in the middle of the parking lot, momentarily drawing the attention away from the building. Its water shot up, forming an umbrella and splattering over.

After dropping Vincent off at his house, Nicholas drove back to town for gas. He'd be running on fumes before long, and the few extra minutes would give his sister more time to adjust to the idea of a stranger coming over. It was the least he could do after springing Sydney's predicament on her.

They passed a handful of places to eat, most small and local, but a few were big-named chains. People bustled in and out, their Friday well on its way. One of the three gas stations shared its building with a fast food restaurant. A tan, older model pickup was stationed at one of the four pumps. Nicholas pulled in behind it, grabbing the spot closest to the entrance.

"You mind if I fill 'er up?" he asked, rolling down the windows and turning off the engine. Sydney shook her head as her stomach growled, rather loudly. She had no idea when she'd last eaten. Nicholas frowned. If the sound had come from anyone else, he might've laughed, but not when it came from the woman next to him. It was just another reminder that whoever she was, she'd had a rough night.

"Let's see," he reached into his pocket and pulled out a twenty dollar bill. "Why don't you guard the pump . . . from the front seat," he said with a wink, "and I'll get us a snack."

Sydney smiled. "Okay."

"What do you want?"

The smiled faded. "I don't know."

"I'll surprise you then. Let's hope you're not picky." He winked again as he got out of the truck.

"Hey, would you mind getting some aspirin, too? The pain reliever they gave me earlier for my headache is starting to wear off."

"Sure thing."

She watched Nicholas set the nozzle in place and head into the store.

What do I want to eat? Am I a picky eater, God?

Praying came so naturally that it gave her the only peace she had in this whole ordeal. It was obvious her memory wasn't completely gone. After all, she knew how to walk and read. She understood and comprehended. She knew things—most things, in fact. She just didn't know the specifics of *who* she was. But the simple fact that she also knew Jesus was a huge encouragement. She felt strangely strong and confident in that memory alone.

A couple minutes later, Nicholas returned with the medicine, two water bottles, two boxes of caramel popcorn, a couple bags of sour cream and onion potato chips, and a pack each of chocolate-covered candies, plain and peanut.

"I took a guess," Nicholas said, handing her the bag. He replaced the nozzle, retrieved his receipt, and restarted the truck. "Well?"

"Um . . . " She raised her eyebrows. "I guess we'll see."

She quickly swallowed two pills before choosing to open the bag of chips and plain candies. She smiled, taking a bite of them together.

"See! You already know what's good. Sweet and salty, just the way I like it, too."

Nicholas pulled into the driveway of a two-story yellow house. A lone tree, full and beautiful in its spring green color, sat off-centered in the front yard, offering shade to over half of the lawn. Shrubs lined the weaving sidewalk leading to the front door with newly planted perennials connecting each green bush.

"Does your sister have any kids?" Sydney asked as she imagined a small neighborhood football game played out on the three-quarters of an acre.

"One. Walker's only a few months old, but he's already the cutest kid in the state." He beamed proudly. "That swing set in the backyard was my gift to him when he was born. I guess it was a little premature, huh?"

She glanced in the direction of his comment, seeing a large wooden swing set in the fenced-in backyard. There were two swings hanging between a green, plastic slide and a set of monkey bars. The whole outdoor toy was covered under a dark, wooden canopy.

"Maybe, but he'll grow into it. It'll be there when he's ready for it, which will be sooner than you realize." Sydney forced a smile.

It felt odd standing in a neighborhood she did not recognize, interacting with someone she had just met, and discussing normal topics of everyday life. She knew she wasn't sick, so to speak, but it didn't fit for her to have the freedom to walk around society when she felt she needed to be surrounded by medical professionals, hooked up to an IV bag or being handed a large pill and a glass of water. She wasn't a picture of health—not mentally, anyway. If she were in a hospital, at least she'd have the mindset that she was being treated for her problem. But she didn't want that either. She chose to leave that place. Here, out in the open, however, she had to keep telling herself it was like a bad nightmare.

They rang the doorbell and a tall, thin woman, holding a towel, opened it. She was cute—the girl-next-door kind of cute. Her light brown hair was pulled back in a low ponytail, and she wore jeans with an orange-and-green-checked blouse.

Her voice was tired but kind as she spoke. "Hey, big brother." She wiped her hands on the towel, drying them. The bags under her eyes were a sign that she'd recently had a baby. She was, no doubt, still in the wake-up-during-the-night stage.

"Hey, sis." He leaned over and gave her a hug. "You sure you don't mind all this?"

She glanced at Sydney and sympathetically responded. "No, not at all. It'll be nice to remember I'm still a nurse, not just a mommy. Though I'm not complaining," she added with a smile. "Come on in."

They stepped into the house. Smells of freshly baked chocolate chip cookies and baby powder greeted them. Classical music played softly from the room to the right.

"Nel, I'd like you to meet someone." Nicholas put his hand on the shoulder next to him. "This is Sydney. Sydney, this is my baby sister, Nellie Yates."

Sydney strained for contentment at the sound of her new name.

"It's very nice to meet you, Sydney, and welcome."

"Thank you. Nice to meet you, too," Sydney said cautiously.

"So," Nellie started compassionately, "how did the two of you actually meet up? I've heard only the basics—that you've lost your memory from a concussion and you're alone." She paused, her mouth slightly turning down. "I am so sorry about that. You must be terrified."

For some reason, talking about her encounters that morning—because she had no idea of who she was—felt embarrassing. It's not like she'd forgotten a test answer or an item at the market. She'd forgotten herself. And what's worse, she didn't know how to go about finding herself. If it'd been a forgotten item from the grocery list, all she'd have to do is go back to the store to retrieve the missing ingredient. Where could she go to get back her memory?

"I, um, I needed some help this morning, and he and his friend offered to be that help. They found me in the woods." She shifted her stance. "Sydney is just a name we thought would work for the time being, since I have no idea what my name actually is." She sighed, showing how exhausted she really was. "I'm okay, I guess—a little tired and dirty, but okay. It's all just very strange."

Nicholas chimed in, momentarily putting to the side the uncertainty of Sydney's morning. *Why was she in the woods? What caused her physical wounds? Why was she alone?* There were no answers yet, and it bothered him. He hoped part of those questions would be figured out soon, but first, he wanted to make sure she was comfortable.

"Nel, other than her staying with you, I was hoping Sydney could also borrow some clothes, if possible. Or I can round up something from Nan's closet while she's away. You all three look to be about the same size."

"No need for that. You know Mom's taste in clothing. It's a bit out there. Sydney is welcome to my closet." Nellie grinned. "How about food? Have the two of you had any today?"

"Not really. I was hoping to sweet talk you into a good, late lunch." Nicholas lovingly winked at his sister.

"Well, no worries," she responded, looking considerately at Sydney. "I haven't eaten yet either. I'll fix us up something while you head upstairs for a shower—or bath, if that's easier." Nellie straightened and slid her hands into her pants' pockets. "I know I've been assigned to keep an eye on you, especially the next twenty-four hours, but I'd like you to feel like you have a say in the matter. Since it's just the baby and me, it gets kind of lonely. It might be nice having another adult around to talk to. But if you'd rather the authorities find someone else for the job, you can say so." Nellie's blue eyes looked sad, but there was a hint of hope in her request. "Whaddaya think?"

Sydney glanced at Nicholas. He was smiling proudly at his sister. If the situation had been reversed, she highly doubted she would've been so generous to help, especially if she had a child. Nellie knew nothing of Sydney. Sydney knew nothing of herself. She hoped she was kind and loving, but she really didn't know. Putting that much trust and faith into a perfect stranger and allowing her into her home was unheard of, wasn't it?

Sydney paused, wondering if it was the right thing to do. Of the limited individuals she'd met today, Nicholas and his sister had been the kindest. If they could trust her, surely she could trust them.

Smiling with hesitant gratitude, she answered, "If you're sure you don't mind."

"Great! It's settled! Nick, why don't you go check on Walker in the den, while I show Sydney around." She put her arm around her brother's guest, completely dismissing the filthy clothes she was wearing. "Come on, Sydney. I'll get out some towels and give you a few options of clothing to choose from."

"I really do appreciate it. It'll be nice to get out of these clothes and start smelling decent again. I know everyone I've seen today would be appreciative, too."

The ladies laughed, as if understanding an inside joke. Nellie led Sydney upstairs to the guestroom as Nicholas thought how blessed he was to have such a trusting and compassionate sister, even after everything she'd been through. He had no doubt the two women would get along beautifully. What time he'd spent with Sydney already testified to their likely compatibility.

1:40 p.m.

"Did you find the girl yet?" he asked, fearful of the answer.

"No! Last time I saw her was when she disappeared into that crowd at the bus terminal. Man! I almost had her, too. Ya think it's poss'ble she got on a bus instead of drivin' off in a car?"

"I doubt it. She didn't look like the type to take a bus." He shifted the phone to the other ear.

"Well, keep your ears low to the ground. No one's lookin' for us at the moment. She'll pro'bly talk, if she ain't already. Don't know what she'd say, though, other than what she saw us do. You're convinced she didn't see our faces; and if that's true, she won't be able to identify us. Kinda hard to pin something on us without an ID."

"It was an accident. Maybe she'll just forget about it and let it go." He tried sounding hopeful.

"Accident or no accident, Roland don't like it when we get sloppy. And he definitely don't like it when there are witnesses."

"Did you tell him about her yet?"

"Nope. Was hoping to take care of her on our own without lettin' him know we messed it up. Just keep an eye out, will ya? Let's don't worry about Roland right now," he nervously suggested. "I'll fill him in soon enough."

2:00 p.m.

The warm shower was just what Sydney needed. She did her best to keep the weight on one leg. Her skin stung as the water rolled down her body, hitting her many cuts. She ignored the sensation. She switched the knob on the showerhead to a higher pressure and tilted her head up. Hard water fell over her face and shoulders, massaging away the tension of the morning. Grime and anxiety washed down the drain, leaving her feeling several pounds lighter. She knew it was imaginary, that a large amount of weight remained—that of her memory. However, she was grateful some of the pressure had been removed.

Careful with her stitches, she finished drying her hair with Nellie's spare hair dryer and hobbled in front of the full-length mirror. It was attached to the back of the closet door. In it, she saw a reflection that seemed familiar, and at the same time, didn't. A woman about five feet, four inches, with sandy blonde hair, a little longer than her shoulders and layered around her face, stared back at her. She was strong-looking, with defined calf and thigh muscles, as if she worked out on a regular basis. Her chocolate-brown eyes seemed almost lifeless after the last several hours. She hoped that would fade in time. Freckles covered her nose and across her cheeks, creating a sort of line just below the frame of her glasses. She noticed her skin was mostly pale, except for the light farmer's tan on her arms and legs, revealing a multi-shaded, skin-colored outline of shorts and a t-shirt.

She pulled herself away from her reflection, hoping that she wouldn't feel like she was looking at a stranger for much longer. Behind her, she noticed a wedding photograph, intricately framed, hanging above the bedpost. Nellie made a beautiful bride. The picture didn't look old, and Sydney secretly wondered why Nellie said it was just she and the baby. What had happened to her husband? She shook her head, reminding herself she had enough to worry about with her own mysteries without needing to understand someone else's.

Several outfits displayed on the bed caught her attention. There was a pair of jeans with a pale purple button-up shirt, a floral skirt and coral top to match, and a mint green pair of sweats. Nellie had given her the option of casual, dressy, or comfortable. Sydney smiled at the thought that went into her choices. It was nice. She didn't know what she would've chosen yesterday, when she knew who she was, but today, she chose casual. She slid on the jeans and shirt and put on a clean pair of socks she pulled from a laundry basket on the floor. She chose not to put her dirty tennis shoes back on. It felt nice to walk, or hop around, without the yuck for a while.

Sydney took one last glance in the mirror on her way out and let out a heavy sigh. She had no choice but to make the most of the opportunity, unless she wanted to wallow her day away. She was grateful for the Nelsons and all they had offered her in the last several hours. At least she could now see and wasn't still in the woods, scared and filthy.

Downstairs, she found Nicholas holding a beautiful, bald, chunky baby. He made faces and cooed at him, trying to get him to smile. Nellie laughed at the two of them while browning some meat on the stove. They were a happy family, though Nellie's happiness seemed sporadic.

Nicholas spun around, seeing the new Sydney. He smiled kindly. "Feel better?"

"Yes, much. Thank you both." She shied away, knowing she was on display, and hobbled to the side of the kitchen.

Nellie looked up from her cooking. "You look nice and refreshed."

"I feel refreshed."

"You like spaghetti?"

"Um, I guess we'll find out." Sydney let out a half-laugh. On the way to the stove, she walked by the baby in Nicholas' arms and smiled. "He's precious, Nellie."

"No arguments here."

"What can I do to help?"

"Nothing. You ought to sit down at the table. Stick your leg on another chair. You've got just enough time to ice that ankle before the venison is ready."

"Okay," Sydney obeyed. Nicholas had an ice pack waiting on her as soon as she situated her leg. She smiled her gratitude. "Venison?"

Nicholas let out a chuckle. "Yep, beats having to buy the meat from the store. It's great; you'll see."

Sydney grimaced. "I'm sure it is."

Nellie laughed and scooped up her son out of his uncle's arms. "You finish browning it, while I feed this little monster." She headed upstairs to nurse him, while Nicholas took over cooking duty.

"So, Nicholas, what do you do? Besides hunt and rescue lost women?" Sydney tried sounding lighthearted as she watched him combine the brown meat with the already-cooked noodles.

"I'm a teacher. And a coach."

"Really? I wouldn't have guessed that."

"And what would you have guessed?" He left the pot of food on the table next to a jar of sauce before pulling three glasses from the cabinet above the dishwasher.

Smiling sheepishly, she said, "Dr. Mitchell said you did odd jobs around the county. So when I heard that, and given that your look is a little, um . . . super casual, I assumed you were a handyman of sorts."

He let out a loud laugh. "I guess I can see how you thought that. Since it's the spring holidays, I've taken a break from shaving. We get about a week-and-a-half off, and I usually spend most of that free time in the woods. The turkeys don't mind a little scruff," he teased. "And yes, I guess I am a bit of a handyman around here. Teachers don't make a whole lot, so I pick up other jobs when I can. Mostly, it's stuff like painting houses or fixing a leaky faucet or yard work. Occasionally, it's even jobs like helping someone move or mending woodwork on a porch railing. Some choose to pay me with money, others with a homemade casserole or pie. I'm generally open to either."

"You sound like a jack of all trades." She opened the jar and mixed in the spaghetti sauce with the meat and noodles, silently wondering why she felt comfortable enough to speak so boldly. "Not to pry, but your truck is pretty nice to have a payday of casseroles and pies."

Goodness, that was pretty insensitive. Thankfully, his expression revealed he hadn't taken it rudely.

"Point taken," he said grinning. "Actually, that's my dad's truck. I drive a very much used, but loved, 2004 Chevy Silverado. Dad flew out to Iowa to visit his brother and his family for a few days. I thought I'd keep it warm for him."

"Very thoughtful of you," she smirked. "What do you teach and coach?"

"Math at the middle school, and I coach the JV boys' soccer team."

"Sounds fun. Bet you're pretty good at both."

"It is fun . . . and rewarding. Wouldn't trade it for all the cubicle jobs in the world." He opened the refrigerator, collecting a plastic jug. "Nellie will want sweet tea. What do you want to drink? She's got tea, milk, diet soda, and water."

"I'll try the tea. Never know if I'll like it unless I try it." She put the lid over the finished spaghetti to keep it warm until they were ready to eat. Nicholas watched her, considering her situation.

"You do realize that you just finished making that spaghetti without asking how. You already knew how."

"I poured sauce over noodles and meat. Walker could have figured that out," she replied sarcastically. "But yeah. Seems I instinctively know most things, maybe even everything. I just don't know myself. It's a blessing, in a way, and at the same time, frustrating that I'm the one thing I can't remember."

"It'll come back. Don't worry," he responded quietly.

"I hope you're right. It'd help if I knew how I got the concussion; maybe then I could start answering questions. I mean, was I playing ball, or did I fall off a ledge somewhere? Was I taking a walk and then slipped on something? Maybe it was as crazy as falling out of bed in the middle of the night. I don't know. I just feel like finding out how I got the concussion would open up the door to figuring out who I am. But then there's the 'I got the concussion by . . . fill in the blank . . . but how did I end up in the woods' question, too." She sighed. "Does any of that make sense?"

Nicholas placed the drinks in front of the plates and took a seat next to her. He leaned over and laid a hand atop hers. "Yes, Sydney, it does." He quickly withdrew his hand, feeling her fingers tighten. She was still a bit apprehensive of him.

She cleared her throat. "I mainly keep wondering how I got here. It's obvious I'm not from around here, since no one seems to recognize me. But if not from here, then where?" She stared at the tiled floor, trying to force the recollections to mind. All that surfaced were more questions.

"You know, when I lose my car keys or my favorite baseball cap—which I do quite regularly—" he admitted with a grin, "I pray. I ask God to help me find them. It's not long before they show up."

He prays? The idea that the hunter who'd found her could be a believer was encouraging.

"Your memory is something lost, just the same as my car keys. In other words, it's around here somewhere." He chuckled, trying to lighten the mood. "If it's His will and if we ask Him, He'll help you find what you lost. Whatcha think?"

Sydney's eyes brightened. She felt the shift from uncertainty to hopefulness as she blinked. It was like someone had thrown a cup of ice cold water in her face to jolt her awake. Hearing Nicholas talk about God brought the picture of a puzzle to mind—different pieces that connect to form a Christian's life. Thankfully, she hadn't forgotten God or His Son, Jesus. They were center pieces of the puzzle. But God's specific Word was another story. She hadn't recalled *why* she knew the Lord, just that she knew and loved Him. Without warning, Bible verses flooded her mind, as if He were talking to her, face to face—verses of His comfort, His peace, His mercy, and His grace. She loved Him, and He loved her—so much so that He sent His only Son to take the punishment for her sins on Himself. He died for her so that she could spend eternity with Him if she believed—and believe, she did. *But whom, exactly, did You die for, Lord? Who am I? What is my name?*

"Sydney?" Nicholas looked concerned. He'd seen her suddenly relax and then stiffen again in confusion.

She shook her head, temporarily clearing away the insecurities. She lifted her eyes to him, the hope returning. "I remember His Word, Nicholas. I remember so many verses. It's beautiful. So yes, Nicholas, let's pray about it."

5:30 p.m.

Vincent spent all day at work, thinking about Sydney. The distractions of his job weren't strong enough to dismiss the events of that morning. The recollection of her piercing, dark brown eyes burned directly into his thoughts. How had she gotten all the way out to Jennings, so deep in the woods? She looked downright lost and terrified when they found her. What had happened to cause that deep cut on the side of her head? She truly didn't know who she was or where she'd come from. At first, he thought she was pretending, messing with them out of fright. However, the more time he spent with her, the more he was convinced her behavior was no act. She really could not remember.

He looked around, trying to find something to do, to take his mind off of her. In order to forget about his morning, he'd needed a full afternoon schedule. Unfortunately, he had no other appointments scheduled that day. Presently, a few dogs were in the back, but they were there only for grooming, not medical purposes.

Being a veterinarian in a small town was busy at times and utterly boring at others. The fact that his clinic was one of two only added to the lack of business. His three assistants took care of all the minor details like running the front desk, filing, and keeping the examining rooms clean. He was only needed when an animal required help. Frankly, the office could probably get by with just two assistants, but the three older ladies had been a part of the clinic long before Vincent took over. He was never sure how to go about downsizing without hurting one of them.

Vincent typically liked his job when it ran smoothly, when the day went by quickly. Unfortunately, today wasn't one of those days. He glanced at his watch. It was five-thirty. He thought about staying and then decided against it. He would cut out a half hour early. If an emergency arose, his assistants would call him. He straightened up the top of his desk and headed out the door, knowing his car would drive itself to Nellie's house. That was where she was—Sydney, the woman who couldn't remember her past.

Vincent Cobb arrived at Nellie's house just as she and Nicholas were stepping out the front door. He pulled his car to the curb, out of the way.

"Hi, guys. Where are you two headed?"

Nellie slid her arm through her brother's. "It's been so long since I've had a night out that Nick here has offered to take his little sister for a bite to eat and then to see a movie. Sydney has graciously volunteered to watch Walker. Truthfully, I think the day has been a bit long for her, and she wanted some time away from me. I've pounded her with questions since she arrived."

"Oh." His expression flattened. "You think that's wise—her watching the baby?" He shrugged, sticking his hands in his pockets. "I mean, what do we know about her? *She* doesn't even know about *herself*. She's a complete stranger. We met her only twelve hours ago."

Nicholas coughed, warning his friend to stand down. Nellie's expression shifted from contentment to annoyance in the blink of an eye.

"Don't you think I've thought about that, Vincent Cobb?" She breathed heavily, offended he didn't respect her motherly instincts, and tried stepping into his territory. Nicholas pulled her back. She unwillingly relented. "I've left her our numbers, and we're not going to be gone long, just a few hours. She's capable, and she won't hurt him."

"How do you know that?"

"I just know, okay?" Her voice reached a higher octave, one that only Vincent pushed her to. "There's something about her. I trust her."

She was tired of her brother's friend always second-guessing her. She shot him a look, the most she could do without upsetting her brother. He finally caught it and stopped pressing her.

Nicholas offered a suggestion. "Sydney's pretty tired, but could probably use some new company—for a few minutes, anyway. That way, you could talk to her, and maybe it'd ease your mind about us leaving Walker with her."

"You think so?" Vincent asked unconvincingly.

"Yeah, sure. Come on. I'll let her know you're here." Nellie let out a *humph* and continued to her brother's truck, while Nicholas walked with Vincent back to the house. He elbowed his best friend and chuckled. "I know you have sense, Vin, but man, when it comes to my sister . . . you're almost a glutton for punishment."

Vincent ground his teeth. "I've got enough sense to know you don't leave a baby with a perfect stranger. And she ought to, too."

"She does, man." Vincent looked over at Nicholas as he heard a touch of humor in his words. "You might want to back off and give Nel the trust she deserves. She's a good mama, and you know that."

The men stepped into the den, spying Sydney sitting on the floor, playing with Walker. The baby's coos brought a gentle smile to her face.

"Thought you left," she said, without looking up.

"Yeah, well, we're trying. Look who just showed up." Sydney turned her attention from the baby to Nicholas' voice. Her smile faded slightly, on impulse. Nicholas ignored the look, hoping his friend had missed it altogether. "You mind if Vin visits with you and Walker for a minute or two?" He leaned in, cupping a hand around his mouth, whispering loud enough for all parties to hear. "I think he's secretly curious about you, maybe even a little worried." He winked.

Sydney repositioned her legs. Her smile returned. "Of course not. It's nice to see you again, Vincent. Please, come on in." She motioned for him to sit in the chair behind where she and Walker had been playing. Then she turned her attention to Nicholas. "Go on. We'll be fine. Enjoy your time with your sister."

"Okay. Have a good evening, Sydney, and make sure you holler upstairs if you need anything," he added as he softly chuckled out the door to rejoin his sister.

Vincent stared at the closing front door in confusion before turning to look at the woman they'd found in the woods just a few hours before. "Who's upstairs?"

"Oh, um, Nellie's sister-in-law. By doctor's orders, I can't be left alone for a while; and it wouldn't be right for Nellie to leave Walker with someone she didn't know, so Kelsey volunteered to . . . I guess . . . babysit us both."

Vincent took a seat, chiding himself for assuming the worse. He brushed his floppy, blond hair out of his eyes. His tall, gangling figure seemed out of place in the petite rocking chair. Sydney let out a quiet giggle.

"You can move to the couch if you'd rather. There's more room. I'll take the chair. I'd like to rock this precious one for a minute or two, anyway."

"Oh, okay." He quickly moved, allowing her to have her way. "Why is Kelsey upstairs?"

"She's editing a few articles for the Jennings paper and said she needed complete quiet. Supposedly, she has a deadline to meet by eight tonight. I'm sure she'll be down to check on us in a few minutes, but I can ask her to come now if you'd like."

Vincent grunted as he shook his head no, inwardly yelling at himself.

When will I ever do the right thing by Nellie?

They sat in awkward silence for several seconds, neither sure of what to say. Sydney studied him, trying to make out why he looked like he was in pain. Vincent Cobb was definitely not as transparent as his best friend.

"You," he finally said, "look clean . . . different . . . nice." He dropped his eyes, somewhat embarrassed.

"Um, thanks, I think." She wasn't sure how to take the man. He seemed nice enough, but his demeanor wasn't as welcoming as Nicholas' and his sister's. "Nellie's been great. She's letting me borrow some of her clothes for the time being."

"Yeah, she's pretty great." He shifted uncomfortably. "You going to stay with her until you figure out what to do?"

"She's offered, and I've accepted. She said she'd like the company and could use the help with the baby for a while. If I'm in the same predicament when she returns to work that I'm in now, I may try to figure out some other arrangements. I definitely don't want to overstay my welcome. Her extended maternity leave is up in two weeks, and Walker will then head to daycare." The thought that her memory could be just as lost two weeks from now was disheartening.

He nodded. "Anything come back to you this afternoon?"

"Yes," she responded, thankful for Who wasn't lost, Who had never left her, even if she'd temporarily forgotten His Word.

"Really?" His eyes widened.

"God did."

"Huh?"

"God did," she repeated. "Well, sort of. I never actually forgot Him; I'd just forgotten the Bible. Now, I'm remembering verse after verse. I don't remember how I know these verses or where I learned them, but I do know them."

Vincent's shoulders slumped. "That's good, I guess." His light blue eyes looked hollow.

"Yes, it's very good," she responded, still trying to figure him out. She'd been around him for only a few minutes throughout the day, but he seemed sad. Some moments, he seemed jumpy and unsure; and others, he came across as cocky and awkward or angrily worried. Those qualities combined spoke of one unhappy with life.

"So, you remember anything else? Your name? Home? Anything?" He asked, looking at the baby now in her arms as she began rocking him.

"Unfortunately, no. Nothing else is coming to me. I'm certain, at least, that Sydney's not my name because every time I hear it, I feel nothing. There's no connection. I have to force myself to listen for the name, reminding myself that she's now me. Sometimes, it takes a few seconds for it to register."

"Understandable. You'll probably be used to it soon enough." He straightened. "You plan on staying until your memory comes back completely, or have you given yourself a time limit on when to move on? You going to go ahead and head out, whether you have your memory or not?"

She looked at him curiously. Was he trying to get rid of her, or was he just making conversation, not realizing how it came across?

"I haven't been able to give it much thought. Right now, you, Nellie, Nicholas, Kelsey, Roberta, and the doctors I met today are the only people I know. I'm not able to look past that at the moment. It's almost too much at once to take in and analyze."

A yawn escaped, bringing out the wear and tear of the day. "I'm sorry, Vincent. It's been a long day, and my sleep deprivation is clouding my thought process."

She leaned over, reaching for Walker's playpen and carefully laid the sleeping boy down. Vincent watched her, wondering how much of what she said was truth. Had she really not thought about her next steps? She seemed awfully calm for someone who was found in the dark, hurt in the woods, without a memory. She acted pretty upset and scared this morning, but now, she's . . . relaxed. Could she have possibly gotten her memory back and is just playing them? He blinked, pushing his suspicions to the back. She was tired; that much he could tell was truth. She yawned again, and he took his cue.

"I'll let you get some rest then. I'm sure I'll see you soon. Good night, Sydney." He stood, running a hand through his hair, and crossed the den to the front door. She grabbed the crutches and followed him.

"Good night, Vincent. And thank you for your help today."

He nodded and walked out, hearing the click of the door lock behind him.

8:15 p.m.

Nicholas enjoyed spending the evening with his sister. He scolded himself for not making more of an effort. She'd struggled throughout her entire pregnancy, knowing that she'd have to raise Walker alone. He'd done as much as he could for her then, even volunteering to move in with her. She accepted all the help he offered, except for that, stating she had to learn how to deal with the nights alone. She knew his staying with her would only be temporary.

But once she'd had his nephew, she seemed renewed somehow, stronger. Nellie put all her energy into her son, which told Nicholas he could start letting her go. He thought back over her excited reaction when he'd mentioned going to dinner and realized he had virtually ignored her while letting her go. He talked to her almost daily, but not in the depths she probably needed. He made a mental note to treat her to dinner, away from Walker, two or three times a month.

He grabbed a handful of popcorn, trying desperately to concentrate on the movie. Instead, Nicholas' thoughts drifted to the conversation he'd had with his buddy from the police department. He'd stepped out and called him during the previews, hoping to hear some good news. Unfortunately, there'd been nothing to report. The deputies had combed the woods and found nothing out of the ordinary. No reports of missing women matching Sydney's description had been filed. There were no findings or suspicions of any nature involving her. His friend promised to contact him if anything came up, but there wasn't much more they could do, other than keep an eye out. It's possible her missing status hadn't even been twenty-four hours yet.

The popcorn stuck in his throat as Nicholas thought of what the pretty, freckled-faced woman was going through. He silently vowed to do everything he could to help her, even if all he could do was pray. For a bachelor, he was suddenly drowning in women trouble.

9:00 p.m.

Sydney decided to put a sleeping Walker to bed, ignoring the feeling that came over her when she was near Vincent. He seemed like two different people at times, and it confused her. She wasn't sure what to make of him just yet—or Dr. Mitchell. Thankfully, Nicholas and his sister were easier to read. The baby's nursery was upstairs, next to the guest bedroom that would become hers for the time being. After Kelsey helped her get Walker upstairs, Sydney laid him on his back in the mahogany crib and wound the mobile above his head. Sports balls of all sorts turned in a circle as a sweet lullaby played softly. Walker didn't move. He slept soundly, feeling safe in his familiar surroundings.

She handed Kelsey the baby monitor and turned out the light. Kelsey would continue to check on them both every twenty minutes, like clockwork.

After the day she'd had, Sydney decided she'd follow the baby's lead, even if sleep came to her in a strange house. And even if she'd be awakened every so often. She sighed. What surroundings were safe and familiar to her? Did she have a house with a crib in it? Were there trees in her front yard, a swing set in the back? Was her house decorated in calming colors like Nellie's, or did she gravitate toward bright, bold colors? Did she even live in a house? Maybe she lived in an apartment. Did she live alone, with her husband, or did she have a roommate whom she carpooled to work with everyday? Surely, she didn't still live with her parents. But then again, maybe she did.

The questions never eased up. They came, one after another, until her head hurt again. She stood at the entranceway to her bedroom, her temporary home. It was painted pale pink and had a single-sized bed against the inner wall. All the furniture was white, girly looking. A short dresser and desk combination sat just beneath the window overlooking the front yard.

The furniture in the guest bedroom was simple and feminine. The larger dresser, adjacent to the shorter one, had a couple of drawers hanging awkwardly. Sydney pulled them out, straightened the metal track underneath, and slid them in properly. Nellie must have pushed the drawers in hurriedly, knocking them off their tracks. She sighed, entirely overwhelmed with the fatigue and unknowns of the day.

God, who am I? I know You know me. I know You love me. But that's about all I know right now. I'm so unbelievably tired, I can't think straight. I'm trying hard to find something to be thankful for—though I am thankful, when I consider where I could be right now without Nellie and her brother. So, thank You for sending them to me. They've been amazingly kind.

Oh God, I'm sorry to complain—I really am—but this day . . . this day has been the longest lasting day. I'm tired because I'm tired, and I'm tired because I'm confused. I feel like I'm walking in a dark tunnel, bumping into everything, not knowing which direction to go. Please, show me where to go, which path to take. Place a light at the end of the tunnel for me to follow. It doesn't have to be a blinding light, just a small one—anything for me to grab on to. Help me to be strong and courageous, not to be terrified through all this.

I don't know who I am, but You do. Help me to remember that. Thank You for being with me. No matter where I'm from or where I go, I know You'll be there every confusing step of the way.

She knew her host would come in and check on her when she returned from her night out with Nicholas. She also knew that Nellie would have to play nursemaid during the night, waking Sydney every few hours. Those were part of the doctor's orders concerning her concussion. She felt bad about that, but her new acquaintance was eager to help. She had a kind heart.

Thanks again for Nellie.

Sydney looked around the room. Nellie's house may not be familiar, but it was safe. She fell on the bed, too tired to get under the covers. Sleep came immediately.

CHAPTER TWO

Friday, April 8

9:00 a.m.

"Good morning, sleepy head." Nellie stopped stirring the big pot on the counter long enough to look at her exhausted guest.

Sydney stretched and yawned. "Morning," she said groggily.

"No crutches?"

"Doesn't hurt near as much." Yesterday's soreness and headache had eased considerably, too.

"That's good news," Nellie replied. "Need to keep it wrapped, though, and elevate it again some today."

"I will," agreed Sydney. "Sorry about last night. I'm sure you must be tired, having to wake me up and all."

"No more than usual. I've got a little one that keeps me up a good bit already, remember?" She nodded in Walker's direction. He was sitting in a bouncy seat near the kitchen table.

"True. But I thank you just the same. You don't even know me."

Nellie gently nodded her head. "Awe, I know you, Sydney. Nicholas told me last night about your conversation with him about Jesus. That's enough for me. If you know Him, then that makes us sisters in Christ." Nellie's eyes didn't seem quite as sad as they had the night before. "I am sorry about Kelsey, though," she added. "I heard she worked on that piece longer than she thought she'd have to."

"Oh," Sydney yawned again, still tired. "There's no need to apologize. She was uh, quiet, but that was fine with me. I didn't mind, really. Walker was just what I needed—a sweet distraction. I guess you could say Kelsey and I both needed our alone time—her with her work and me with my thoughts, since that cute baby of yours doesn't talk back."

She peeked over at the silent partner. He'd found the seatbelt across his stomach fascinating.

"So, what are you making at nine o'clock in the morning?" She leaned over, sniffing the meal's aroma. "Smells delicious."

"I hope you'll like it. It's Brunswick stew. I'm making enough for our dinner tonight and for leftovers. I've even got enough for any straggling visitors that decide to stop in and check on their mystery lady." She sent a gleam over her shoulder.

Sydney ignored the look, but couldn't help the grimaced expression that silently responded across her own face. "I look forward to trying it."

Nellie smirked, noting her houseguest didn't like to be teased early in the morning. "There's some cereal in the pantry, unless you'd rather have eggs and bacon?"

"Uh," she glanced at the food closet. "I guess I'll give the cereal a go. Where are the bowls?"

"Try the dishwasher. I haven't unloaded it yet."

Sydney grabbed a glass bowl and spoon. She found a box of bran cereal in the pantry and retrieved the milk out of the refrigerator. Before she sat down to eat, she turned on the music above Walker's head. It had stopped, and he looked like he was reaching for it. The lights on the bouncy seat's handle were set in time to the music it played. His legs kicked in excitement.

She silently thanked the Lord for her food. She'd hoped to wake with some more of her memory. She hadn't. She tried not to let that bother her, though she knew she'd fail. A memory is something that is a part of you. Without it, nothing, including life itself, felt right. It was like she was playing a part in a movie or reading about a character in a book. She wondered when the last page would appear.

Nellie set the crockpot to low and put the lid over the stew. She picked up her cup of coffee off the counter.

"Would you like some coffee?" she asked.

"Yes, that would be nice."

"How would you like it? Or do you want to try it a few different ways? Black? Cream and sugar?" She poured the coffee into a large, green mug.

"For some reason, I want to say black."

"Well, if you like it black, then I'd say that's a good sign—if that's what your subconscious is telling you. It's something, anyway." She handed Sydney her cup and took a seat next to her.

"You eaten?"

"A couple hours ago. I thought about waiting, but changed my mind once my stomach growled loud enough, I thought it'd wake you."

Sydney chuckled and took a bite of her cereal. She wasn't sure she really liked it, but she didn't want Nellie to feel like she had to make her anything else. She looked up and saw an envelope on the edge of the kitchen table. It had her name on it, or, at least, her name for the time being.

She pointed. "What's that?"

Nellie reached over and handed it to her. "It's an envelope of two or three restaurant gift cards. The two of us have been instructed to go lunch hopping, but only if you feel up to it. And only if you use your crutches while we're out."

"Lunch hopping?"

"Yep. We don't have a lot to choose from around here, but maybe we can find something you like to eat. Get a hamburger at one place and a dessert at another kind of thing."

Sydney put down her spoon and reached for the envelope.

"Is this Nicholas' doing?"

"He's a bachelor, Sydney. He needs someone to spend his money on every once in a while. Otherwise, he ends up buying silly little gadgets for his desk at school." She laughed. "He's a kid at heart, which makes him the coolest teacher around. Most teachers come across as stiff and boring; kids can't wait to get out of their classes. Not Nicholas' students. They love his class and his style of teaching because he's a lot like his desktop—crazy and unique. He'll change the items out every once in a while to keep their attention. Usually the trinkets will have something to do with the lesson; maybe a bit far-fetched, but Nick makes it work."

Sydney was intrigued, and she hadn't even seen his desk. "What kind of things?"

"Well, let's see," Nellie continued, remembering her brother's habits growing up. He'd done the same thing on his desk in his bedroom, but back then, they were only army figurines. "They could be math boxes, where the kids have to figure out some ridiculously hard puzzle, or some ticking mechanism, where they have to estimate the number of ticks per minute or the pattern of the ticks. Whatever it is, even if it's temporarily a superhero action figure, it always gets the students motivated and wanting to come back to math class the next day."

Nellie grinned. "Nicholas has this saying, 'Love the Lord and enjoy life.' He lives by it. Makes the most of opportunities. He has fun and tries to keep a positive attitude while bringing God glory with his life. The kids—they get that he's different. They want to be like him, so he rarely has trouble getting them to pay attention in class or to do their homework." She looked down at her son, still kicking his feet. "You know, that crazy desktop habit of his—whether it be Superman with a division sign across his chest in place of the 'S' or an algebraic equation made out of mini Oreos—actually helps keep his class functioning smoothly."

Sydney laughed. For some reason the partial description of Nicholas' superhero approach to classroom management fit what she already knew about him. He was friendly, outgoing, and a hero, of sorts, to her.

"So," Nellie continued, "whaddaya say? You up for a little taste testing? We won't be gone long, just about an hour or so. Kelsey likes to spend a few hours with Walker every week, usually while I run errands. But since she was so preoccupied with work last night, she volunteered to watch him as soon as I mentioned the possibility. Please," she pleaded.

Sydney took a sip of her black coffee. It was good. "Okay. Sure, sounds kind of fun. And then later this week, if you still need to run those errands, I'd be happy to watch Walker for you, if I'm still here."

"Perfect!"

CHAPTER THREE

Saturday, April 9

10:00 a.m.

Sydney subconsciously reached for the tennis shoes under her bed. Nellie had been kind enough to wash them for her. The shoes were Sydney's definition of comfort. She had a feeling she was the type who would choose a pair of tennis shoes every day of the week. She knew she'd wear them with a Sunday dress, if she could get away with it. She slid the shoes on over the compression bandage that seemed unnecessary now and pulled her hair back into a tight ponytail. A few of the layered strands around her face refused to cooperate, flying wildly and without care.

She didn't know why, but she wanted to get outside. She wanted the fresh air. After letting Nellie know where she'd be, Sydney left the safe haven of her new friend's house. She didn't venture too far away from Nellie's, afraid she'd eventually get lost. Instead, she strolled the loop in front of the house.

Even though Sydney moved slowly, something about foot to pavement seemed routine. Her feet struck the pavement at a snail's pace, but in rhythm, as if to music. It felt natural. A gentle breeze mixed with the morning's rising temperatures drove her forward. Somehow, she knew the experience was a sign of familiarity, of security.

Time passed. Her glasses hung loose on her nose, causing her to take them off and hold them, walking into a blurry, but enjoyable, unknown. She felt sweat drip down her back, loving every drop.

Sydney knew what the light exercise had done to her body. She knew she was once again very dirty. But this time, it was different. This time, she felt cleansed from the sweat and heat. Momentarily, she felt the fear release through her pores. Her mind was just as confused as it'd been before she left the house. Her memory was still missing. She was just as lost mentally; but in that moment, she felt free. She was free to be lost, free to be confused. She easily pushed the anxiety of her circumstance to the side and breathed in the freedom she knew exercise brought her. Sydney knew deep down that if she ever needed to clear her mind, this was how she did it, but on a much higher level. She knew deep down that she was a runner.

5:30 p.m.

Nicholas was going over to his sister's house for dinner for the third night in a row. He'd spent the remainder of his spring holiday searching the woods where they'd found Sydney, looking for answers, answers that the Jennings Police Department couldn't find. He looked for someone else who may be lost or hurt. He looked for tracks of some sort, clues of how she'd ended up where she did. He'd located broken twigs that followed a fairly straight path, near where he found her. It was possible she stumbled in the dark, hitting the limbs as she walked. She'd told him there were scratches on her arms and legs and a few on her stomach. The stiff twigs poking out and the briars nearby could've caused some of those scratches.

Other than the bent wood, he found nothing else helpful. It had rained that first night Sydney was at Nellie's, and in turn, washed away any possible leads. No one else was found in the woods, so Nicholas assumed she was alone. When he wasn't in the woods, looking for clues, he was on the Internet. He searched for stories of disappearing individuals in the state of Georgia. Unfortunately, there were quite a few. The police told him there wasn't a whole lot they could do that he wasn't already doing. As far as they knew, no crime had been committed. They'd keep a look out and check connections that Nicholas didn't have. If anything came up, they agreed to contact him.

He hadn't told Sydney what he was doing yet. She had enough on her mind with the day-to-day living. She tried hard to make herself remember. After awhile, that straining caused her headache to return, and Nellie would convince her to try doing something normal like watching a movie or taking a nap—anything to get her mind to relax.

Over the last two days, Sydney had remembered bits and pieces. She remembered God's Word, which went a long way in helping her cope. She remembered she liked black coffee and running. She also remembered her favorite color was purple, and she wasn't much of a reader.

Nicholas stepped into his sister's home, where he found Vincent in the den, pacing and mumbling, seemingly angry at something.

"Hey, buddy. What's up?" Nicholas closed the door behind him.

Vincent stopped pacing. His eyes transformed from gray to a cloudy blue. "Nick. I didn't hear you come in."

"I noticed. Where're the girls?" he asked, looking down the short hall leading to the kitchen.

"Um, upstairs. Sydney and Walker were taking a nap. Nellie went to wake them both."

"Oh." Nicholas sat on the couch. "You okay, Vin? You look . . . upset."

Vincent shrugged, waving him off. "I'm fine. It's nothing. No big deal."

"If you say so." Nicholas eyed him curiously. Normally, Vincent wasn't a man of many words, but he typically confided in Nicholas. However, something had him twisted up enough that he wasn't even going to let his best friend know about it.

Nicholas scratched his head. "You here for dinner?"

"No . . . yes . . . I don't know." Vincent shook his head, indecisively.

"Relax, man. It was a simple question." He motioned for him to sit at the other end of the couch. "Take a seat."

Vincent complied. He was awfully jittery for a Saturday night. He usually mellowed by this time of the week, knowing the weekend meant fewer work hours. He glanced at the floor, unsure how to answer Nicholas' question. He'd originally come by to check on Sydney, to talk with her alone. Knowing she was still staying under Nellie's roof, he wanted to see if there'd been any progress with her memory. Now, seeing they'd be surrounded, he wasn't sure he wanted to stick around and find out.

A throat cleared to the right. Nellie, Walker, and a sleepy Sydney stood staring at the men. They looked as if they were waiting for something, an answer to an unknown question. Sydney seemed puzzled, almost gawking at Nicholas.

Nicholas stood. He no longer sported the grizzly bear appearance. He was clean-shaven. His Adam's apple was clearly visible, as was his chin, square and strong. The fresh look enunciated his eyes. They were blue, bright, and brilliant—a contrast to Sydney's dark brown ones. His chestnut-colored hair was cut short, professional-looking. The five-foot-eleven-inch stance seemed taller than it had yesterday. He wore a dark pair of jeans and an ocean blue vest over a paler blue button down shirt. Without all the camouflage, his strength and defined physique stood out. The hunter was definitely handsome when he cleaned up.

"Do I have something on my face?" he asked Sydney as he jokingly wiped away an invisible piece of dirt.

She blinked, shaking her head. "No, not anymore." She studied him a second longer. "You know, I had no idea that face was under all that hair," she teased.

"That was only a week-and-a-half worth of growth. Nothing but a shadow. Stick around long enough, and you'll see what I look like at the end of summer break. Now, that's a sight."

"As interesting as that sounds, I hope that if I'm here that long, it's by choice, not by mere survival." She rubbed her eyes, forcing them to remain open and giving herself a half second to disguise the despair that washed through her at the thought she'd *need* to be in Jennings that long.

"And a beard in the heat of summer? Really?"

He nodded and smiled gently. "To each his own."

Nicholas studied Sydney's reaction. He'd caught the glimmer of fear that flashed across her eyes, but then disappeared just as quickly. She handled her memory loss amazingly, able to joke and create friendships. She was a strong woman. He wouldn't mind getting to know her better—if time and circumstances allowed.

"Well, gentlemen," Nellie said cheerfully, "I don't want to cook. So, what are you two going to do about that, assuming you are both here to eat?"

"Is that so? And what about you, Sydney? Would you like to do the cooking?" Nicholas grinned.

"Only if you want a grilled cheese sandwich. I'm afraid that's about the extent of my cooking abilities."

"You helped with the spaghetti the other night."

"Funny. Pouring sauce over meat does not a cook make. That's something else that's come back to me—my shortcomings in the culinary department."

Vincent took in a deep breath. Her memory *was* coming back, slowly.

Nicholas put his hand on Vincent's shoulder. "Well, Vin, I guess that leaves the two of us taking the two of them, plus the munchkin, out to eat. What do you say?"

Vincent forced a smile. "I say . . . pizza it is."

6:00 p.m.

The pizza restaurant was loud. Saturday night in a small town meant teenagers—lots of them. They were out in droves, trying to enjoy what was left of their spring break. Vincent seemed nervous, a bit edgy for some reason. There was something weighing heavily on his mind. Nicholas, on the other hand, seemed comfortable and very content in his element. He was having a wonderful time, making the most of his last days of freedom as much as the students were.

"Hey, Coach Nelson!" a boy, about thirteen, hollered across the room. He sat with a few other friends at one table, while his parents occupied another.

"Hey there, Eddie. You ready to get back at it bright and early Monday morning?" Nicholas pointed to his eyes and then to Eddie's, gesturing that he had his eyes on him.

The group of boys laughed, and all nodded. Sydney saw what Nellie had talked about earlier. Her brother had a way with the kids that demanded respect and fun at the same time. She admired him for that.

A waitress brought a pitcher of soda and one of water for the table.

"Y'all mind if I just leave these here? If not, it might take a while to refill your drinks." She smacked her gum and looked around the room. "It's, like, crazy in here tonight."

Nellie smiled. "Not at all. We understand. Tell you what, if it'll help, why don't you just bring us two pizzas of whatever's easiest and fastest to make. We'll try to be out of your hair as soon as we can." She eyed the large group of girls walking through the door. "Looks like you're going to need our table pretty soon."

"Sounds good to me," Nicholas chimed in.

"All right. See what I can do." She walked off toward the kitchen.

Walker started crying. Nellie rocked his car seat on the floor, unable to soothe him. She pulled his pacifier out of her purse and quickly put it into his mouth. That did the trick for the moment.

"I forgot about it being spring holiday and a Saturday night combined. Walker may not last very long. I hate to miss our night out, but if he gets fussy, would one of you mind driving me home? I don't want everyone's night to be ruined because of this." They'd taken both men's vehicles because the five of them, with Walker's car seat, couldn't fit comfortably into Nicholas' truck. He still hadn't unloaded all the hunting equipment.

Vincent responded, "I'll take you. I've got some things to do around my house anyway."

He wouldn't get his chance to talk to Sydney tonight, but he wasn't about to miss a chance to spend time with Nellie. She'd been the love of his life since high school. There wasn't anything he wouldn't do for her. She, however, saw him only as Nicholas' best friend, another brother, in a way. He'd tried talking her out of dating some of the not-good-enough-for-her men in college and out of marrying Ken, when he found out he had a dysfunctional family, but she never listened. Everything he did was for her, to protect her. If he couldn't be her husband, he determined to be a good friend.

6:30 p.m.

Vincent pulled the base of the car seat out of Nicholas' truck and placed it in his vehicle. Nellie was right. The baby hadn't lasted long. The restaurant was too much stimulation for him, and he was inconsolable after fifteen minutes of arriving. They had to get their pizza to go.

Nellie sat in the back with her son. She was always cautious around Vincent, careful not to give him the wrong idea. She'd known how he cared about her ever since her brother had told her several years ago. She normally wouldn't have ridden with him by herself, but she didn't know a way around the situation without disrupting a much-needed night out. It'd been a trying week for all of them, especially Sydney. By her facial expressions and body language, Nellie knew Sydney was uncomfortable around Vincent, so she didn't feel right leaving him with her.

"You doing okay, Nellie?" Vincent asked, staring straight ahead. "I mean, with everything?"

Nellie's husband, Ken, had died suddenly a few months after they were married. A week after the funeral, she found out she was pregnant. That first half-year was rough on everyone in the family, but especially Nellie. She battled temporary depression, and he and Nicholas feared the baby wouldn't survive.

Nellie gently ran a finger down her son's arm. All his fussing at the restaurant had worn him out. He'd fallen asleep as soon as they'd driven off.

"I'm fine." She knew why he was asking, but she wished he wouldn't. Nicholas pried and fretted enough for the both of them. She didn't need two big brothers.

"Good." He responded, a bit too quickly. He really just wanted to get to what bothered him, while he had her alone. "Are you enjoying having Sydney around, even though you don't really know anything about her?"

"Don't start, Vincent," Nellie bellowed in frustration, but not too loud for the sake of her sleeping son. "She's fine. She's a good person, and yes, I'm enjoying having her around. She's been a big help with Walker, and it's been nice to have someone to talk to other than Nicholas." She spoke without a breath between sentences, reminding him to tread the unwelcomed water carefully.

He shifted positions on the steering wheel, squeezing the rubber until his knuckles turned a shade lighter. He hadn't gotten his chance to feel Sydney out earlier; but if he was cautious, maybe he'd get the information he wanted out of Nellie. His antics of protecting her usually annoyed her. She typically shut him down before he could get in his opinion of a situation.

He cleared his throat. "I'm glad. Seems like the two of you are getting along okay."

"We are."

"And Walker likes her?"

"He does."

"Have you been able to find anything in common, with her memory gone and all?"

"Yes."

"Like what?"

"Most everything."

She wasn't making it easy on him. She didn't seem to have any intention of offering anything useful. He took a deep breath. He'd have to come right out and ask.

"What is she remembering besides that she's not a cook?" He tried to sound disinterested, like he was only making small talk.

"Things she likes and doesn't like, feelings mainly. Some specifics have come back, but not anything that'd lead us to her identity. So much has come to mind, though, over the last few days that I'm pretty confident it won't be much longer, and she'll know who she is. She'll remember everything soon enough."

Vincent swallowed hard, feeling an invisible cloud of doom form over him.

8:00 p.m.

Sydney left the restaurant hopeful for what the coming days might bring. While eating a slice of pepperoni pizza, she'd had her first real memory of an actual event in her past. It came to her so abruptly, she nearly choked on her food.

She was ten, sitting next to a man—her dad. They were both dressed in black. Although they'd both been crying, they suddenly laughed at something. Another man swung pizza dough in the air. He tossed it around and around, getting higher with each toss. Someone from across the room hollered, and the man turned to look. He took his eyes off the flying dough for one second. That's all it took. The gooey, uncooked bread came down quickly, landing directly across her father's face. Sydney's ten-year-old self laughed so hard that she forgot for one minute why she'd been crying, why they'd both been crying. She forgot momentarily that she was trying to eat lunch after her mother's funeral.

Though the memory was from a long time ago, it still brought a strong feeling of sadness with it. Her expression wore mixed emotions. She was devastated all over again at the loss of her mother, even if she couldn't remember anything about her. She remembered the connection she had with her, the happiness of knowing her. Yet she was also excited and encouraged. An actual memory had come to her. She wasn't just some stranger no one knew. She had a mother and a father. She had laughed, and she had cried.

Sydney shared her news with Nicholas, certain he'd take the information in stride and with sensitivity. Over the last couple of days, he'd lovingly poked fun at her when she needed a lift and patiently listened when deep subjects needed to be thought through or talked through. He kindly observed the likes and dislikes that explained part of who she was and never discouraged or disbelieved her when those observations were a result of a *feeling*, not an actuality.

Nicholas listened to her story of an afternoon spent in a pizza parlor and smiled gingerly.

"That's great, Syd. You remembered something—something important. You remembered your parents." He got out of the truck to open Sydney's passenger side door. They moved slowly up the walkway to Nellie's front entrance. "I'm sorry about your mom," he said quietly. "That's a hard memory."

"Thank you. I know I was just a little girl, but . . . it hurt; it still hurts. Is that crazy?"

"No, not in the least. If it still hurts, then it means you had a loving mother. You had a good relationship with her."

"Yeah, I guess you're right." She watched her feet as they walked. Thankfully, her ankle had quit bothering her completely.

"Your memory also tells me you had a loving father and a good relationship with him, as well." She looked up at him, interested in his interpretation. "If you were eating pizza, usually a child's favorite food, on the day of your mother's funeral, that tells me he was trying to console you. He was upset himself and could've gone home and disappeared into his own room. Instead, he took his precious daughter out for pizza. He put your needs above his own. He knew you needed to eat and to be comforted just as much as he did."

Nicholas stopped in front of the door. "You know, I think your memory also reveals something about your younger years. If I had to guess, Sydney, I'd say you had a good childhood, a happy one."

"How so?" she asked, curiously.

"Well, assuming you learned about Jesus from your parents, that in itself is the foundation of a good childhood. But the fact that you were able to laugh on that sad day, to laugh with your father, turning your tears momentarily into smiles, tells me that, too. Any family that is centered in Christ and can laugh is a good one. It's a great one, one to be proud of. I can only hope and pray I'll be blessed with a family like that of my own one day."

"Don't you have that kind of family now? You and Nellie are exactly what you just described. The two of you love God and are constantly smiling and enjoying life."

"I have that with Nellie, for the most part, but only Nellie. My parents don't know the Lord. We've tried talking to them, but they've shut us out, especially Dad. He basically leads their decisions—together in every opinion. They don't want to hear us. Dad's eyes harden, looking ice cold if the topic of God ever comes up. So to keep communication open, Nellie and I decided to stop pushing, so to speak, God on them. All we can do at this point is pray and live by example."

"I'm so sorry, Nicholas." Sydney struggled to picture the description of his parents.

"We come across to everyone in town like the perfect family. We did laugh a lot growing up. There wasn't a shortage of that, which I'm grateful for. But laughter without God in your life is just smiles and noise. With God, with what comes with Him, with salvation and the promise to never be separated from Him for all eternity, now that is so much more. That's *joy*. And joy runs deep. Nothing can rob you of your joy, not even the death of a beloved mother." His shoulder bumped hers in a friendly gesture.

Sydney stared at him in awe. His outward playfulness was his shell. Inside, Nicholas Nelson was a deep-seated man with heart-wrenching convictions and a love for others, especially his own family. How could she have ever been frightened of him, even with the grizzly look? She smiled at her own thought.

"I guess I do feel pretty strongly that my parents taught me about Jesus. It just seems right, you know?" Sydney returned his shoulder bump. "And true, you're right, my mom's death didn't take away my joy; nothing can—not even my memory loss. I know I'll see her again. And whether or not I'll have my complete memory back, well, I guess that's up to God. Either way, He's given me Him, and as you said . . . He is my joy." She reached for the knob, paused a moment, then turned back to look at him.

"Nicholas?"

"Yeah?"

"Do me a favor. Remind me of that fact when I let my situation get the best of me."

"Sure thing." He grinned, admiring the woman before him even more.

CHAPTER FOUR

Sunday, April 10

5:30 a.m.

He paced back and forth, unable to sleep, burning an imaginary hole in his carpet. It'd been over three days since they'd tried making the trade. He knew his boss Roland was particular and had his hand in numerous criminal ventures, from gambling and racketeering to money laundering to illegal drugs and pharmaceuticals. He ran each aspect of his crime syndicate separately so that each employee stuck to a specialty. There was no crossover.

Roland's operation had clearly proven lucrative over the years, and his reputation had expanded. Although a select few had met him face to face, the name *Roland* was immediately appreciated and feared throughout several communities across the country. That fear kept him in business. No one dared to attempt to actually locate him or rat him out—mainly because of what he'd do, but also because they didn't want to lose what he offered.

As in all aspects of his operations, Roland had stuck with the simple and specific in his illegal prescription drug sale, keeping those involved to a minimum. He was a meticulous planner. He had only a small number of suppliers and a particular repeat group of buyers. He used two runners or middlemen for every transaction—one to pick up from the supplier and one to hand off to the buyer. And when a

75

new supplier or buyer was added, he or she was chosen carefully after thorough research. This business reasoning was one of patience, allowing the time needed to grow and succeed, to move at a snail's pace. "Slow and steady wins the race" was his motto.

It was clear Roland liked control; and because of the nature of his investment—the tedious and careful planning—he wasn't a man to be reckoned with. Roland was smart and hard and callous. He had a lot riding on every detail of his investment, from beginning to end.

Roland always did his research, no matter how long it took to get the answers. The places he chose to make exchanges were inconspicuous and private. If they'd just followed Roland's orders and met where he'd instructed, none of this would've happened. No one would've gotten hurt. One did not cross him and get away with it.

He stopped pacing and sat down, dropping his head into his hands. His own job fell under pharmaceuticals—supplier—which he'd have thought would've been the safest of Roland's endeavors. He had to personally interact with only one other individual, securing an *I'll tell on you if you tell on me* policy. One person's word against another's. No one else was ever around. It was easy. Supply the drug from his office, and hand it over. In and out—nothing to it. But this time was different.

His partner convinced him to meet in the middle of the night at a superstore instead of their usual location, and he'd promised that Roland was good with this change of plans. That should've been a clue. He knew Roland never risked a plan change at the last minute.

At ten after one in the morning, they were to meet in the electronics department. No one was scheduled to work that section of the store between one and three, stationing employees at more needed spots during the night. It should've been a simple job, one a child could've pulled off. All they had to do was meet, the supplier handing over the package in exchange for a cash payment. The whole thing shouldn't have taken more than twenty seconds.

Instead, he caught his partner cutting cables that tied down computer tablets and stuffing the electronics into a book bag. He debated skipping the meet after spotting what he knew to be a personal, not-a-part-of-the-plan theft. But the consequence of bailing would be great. So he chose to wait and watch, hiding in the background. When the cutting and snatching ceased, he made his way to the man and proceeded with the exchange.

Everything went according to plan, until he saw *her*. She'd picked up a Nikon D7100, studying it. She looked through the lens, in their direction, just as the other man finished checking the drugs for authenticity. There wasn't anyone else around. No one would specifically be able to tell what they were doing. No one, that is, except her. Although she was a good forty feet away, the lens she looked through gave her just enough magnification to see exactly what they were doing.

He'd hoped she wasn't paying them any attention or had misinterpreted their movement. The quiet gasp he'd heard told him differently. She'd seen them and understood exactly. She knew what they were doing. He would've let her go. He wanted to let her go. The man beside him, on the other hand, had no intention of letting anyone go. As soon as he heard the gasp, he looked up and caught sight of the woman, staring at them in horror. He'd go after her if she didn't run.

The exchange was no longer worth it. His partner suddenly looked sweaty and began to panic. "Let's go!" he'd growled out, dropping to shove the drugs in with the tablets into the book bag. "I ain't riskin' bein' caught. You'll get your money later."

It all happened in the blink of an eye. They were so focused on the girl's gasp and the sudden need to escape that neither noticed the employee who'd walked up behind them.

The man finished stuffing the package of drugs into the book bag and stood quickly, swinging the book bag hard over his shoulder. Instead, it hit the employee that had, by then, made his way between them. The bag knocked the scrawny teenager across the chest, pushing him backwards. He didn't weigh much more than a hundred pounds. He stumbled, throwing his arms in the air, trying to catch his balance. His head came crashing down on the corner of the cashier's counter behind them, and he fell the rest of the way, limp. A thick pool of gut-wrenching blood gathered under his head. Two round, blank eyes stared at them, condemning yet seeing nothing. They heard another gasp.

The woman hadn't run when they caught her spying. She'd stayed. And now she'd also witnessed something much worse. It was accidental, but still. He wished she'd left before. Why hadn't she gone after she was spotted? Why hadn't she run then? The man with him might've been convinced to let her go over the first incident, but murder . . . that's a different story. As bad as he figured his associate to be, Roland was crueler. He'd be furious with them for botching the job; but when he found out there was a witness, there was no telling what Roland would do.

9:45 a.m.

Nicholas pulled into his sister's driveway. He'd promised to take Nellie, Walker, and Sydney to church and then on a picnic. The weather predicted to be perfect for an afternoon of fun in the sun. Sydney walked downstairs, catching Nicholas' attention. He thought her breathtaking. She wore a green and yellow floral dress that hung low to her ankles with nude-colored heels. Her hair was down, pulled slightly behind her ears, and her face showed contentment. The little makeup she wore accentuated her eyes, even her freckles. A slight grin crossed his face as he noticed her nose crinkling in discomfort.

"Good morning, Sydney," he smiled. He wanted so much to tell her she looked beautiful, but he couldn't, not yet. He didn't know if he had a right to. She could very likely be a married woman.

"Morning, Nicholas." She pushed the glasses up her nose. "I know I've been preoccupied, but that doesn't excuse my behavior."

"What behavior would that be?" he asked, intrigued.

"I never thanked you for the gift cards."

"Oh, that. No big deal."

"It was a lot of fun restaurant hopping, as Nellie called it. You managed to turn my memory loss into a game, I guess you could say." She shifted uncomfortably. "It's hard to explain, but being able to taste test different foods within that short time frame made me feel productive. I got to figure out what I liked quickly, instead of waiting from meal to meal. Silly, I know. But it was a step taken toward an identity. I felt less like a hypothetical and more like an individual for a moment. So, thank you."

"You're welcome. Food preferences are essential," he winked. "And might I add, your preference in my sister's clothes is spot-on." He smiled. He may not be able to tell her she was beautiful, but he could find other ways to pay her compliments.

She grabbed the edges of her dress and twirled around. "Why, thank you."

The church service was just what she needed. Most of the town folk had heard of the new girl with the missing memory. They were sympathetic and kind, as well as a little curious. Sydney could've done without the curiosity, but she was grateful for the obvious acceptance. The worship part was deep and meaningful, filling the sanctuary with beautiful voices. She enjoyed singing praises to her Lord. It prepared her heart for what God had to say through the pastor and His Word.

The elderly man preached from Matthew six, a chapter from Jesus' Sermon on the Mount. The verses spoke to Sydney, especially verses thirty-three and thirty-four: "But seek first his kingdom and his righteousness, and all these things will be given to you as well. Therefore do not worry about tomorrow, for tomorrow will worry about itself. Each day has enough trouble on its own."

She thought about those words, letting them linger long after the service had ended. God was reminding her that He saw the big picture. He saw the outcome of her situation. She was given a view only of what was directly in front of her. Her job wasn't to see what He saw. She needed to trust Him with that. Her job was to seek Him; to daily come to Him for guidance; to put Him above herself, her worries, and her concerns. If she did that, she could be at peace. She needed to take it one day at a time, thanking Him for the blessings and provisions He'd given her. There was no need to fret about the what-ifs. Easier said than done.

Sydney did trust God. She knew He'd see her through and restore her memory if He wanted. But she couldn't help feeling strange about the whole thing. She couldn't quite put her finger on the feeling exactly. She was calm, for the most part—probably strangely calm—certain that she didn't need to worry about tomorrow, that she just needed to face the day she was living. However, at the same time, something gnawed at her, something that she felt would come into play on a tomorrow, one day soon. She tried to ignore the unusual feeling in the pit of her stomach. It did her no good to dwell on it or make herself sick trying to figure out where it was coming from.

Nicholas carefully came up behind Sydney.

"Hey, you okay?" he asked, concern filling his voice. "You look like you're halfway across the country."

"Oh." She chuckled. "Sorry. I'm fine. Just chewing over what was said this morning. I enjoyed your church very much. Thanks for inviting me."

"Glad you came. I think the locals felt like they had a real-life celebrity in their midst." He winked.

"Yeah, I got that. They're very kind, though." She smoothed out her dress, wiping off a piece of lint. "Nellie getting the baby?"

"Yes. She should be here in a sec. The nursery isn't very crowded today. Some of the families with school-aged siblings are probably still on vacation from the break. Next Sunday, we should have a full house."

"If I'm around next week, I'd like to see that. Maybe by then, my celebrity status will have worn off a bit," she added, smiling somewhat sadly.

"You can count on it . . . seeing a full house, that is. Your celebrity status may take longer than a week or two to fade away. It's a small town. We tend to jump on anything new and hold on to it until the next new thing comes around. Your best bet is to hope a talking camel is caught walking down Main Street."

Sydney laughed, but felt a deep-seated uncertainty. What if the next new thing still had something to do with her?

1:00 p.m.

"Nick, can you pass the potato salad?" Nellie asked.

"That's your third helping. Hungry much?" he teased.

"Why, yes, as a matter of fact, I am. Now, give it here before I threaten to take away your rights to open dinner invitations." She snatched the bowl of potato salad out of his hands.

Nicholas had thought of everything for the picnic. He'd brought two blankets to sit on, a typical brown basket filled with plastic utensils and paper plates, sodas, a small cooler for the cold foods, and another cooler for the warm foods. He'd even taken care of the dessert. That, he made himself. It was a delicious pecan pie. The other food—the apple slices, potato salad, fried chicken, green beans, corn on the cob, and rolls—were from the home-style cooking restaurant across the street from their church. He'd purchased the food after the service and transported it over to the coolers for that picnic-feel.

"Syd, how is it?" Nicholas asked, stuffing half a roll into his mouth.

She swallowed a bite of corn as she wiped her mouth with a red-and-white-checked napkin. "Too good to stop eating and answer you."

He laughed. "That's what I like to hear. Eat up and enjoy!" He turned his attention to his sister.

"What time does Walker need to be back for his nap?"

Nellie glanced at her watch. "He usually goes down around one-thirty or two, but I doubt he'll make it that long. Sundays are rough on him. He spends his mornings looking around at all the different people. It wears him out."

"Oh."

"Don't worry, big brother," she said with a laugh. "I'm not about to ask you to take us home early. Not after all the work you put into this picnic. If he gets grumpy, he can cry it out. We're outside. He's not going to bother anyone but us. After a few minutes of crying, he'll fall asleep. A nap in the sunshine will be good for him."

"Great." He picked up another piece of chicken. "It's too pretty to have to go inside."

"Agreed," she smiled. "Oh, Sydney?"

Sydney looked up from her almost empty plate. "Yes?"

"I've been thinking. If things don't change and if your memory is still missing when I go back to work next week, I'd love for you to continue as things are." She paused, taking a quick sip of her lemon-lime soda. "I don't have to send Walker to daycare, not yet anyway. You're welcome to stay and watch him for me, if you'd like. I'll pay you, of course."

Sydney put her fork down. "Room and board is plenty pay. But won't you lose his spot? What if there's not another opening when or if . . . " She slowly blinked, dragging out the word, " . . . it does come back. That's not fair to you or Walker."

"Oh, well, I thought about that and called them with that same question. The lady didn't seem to think it'd be a problem. True, she couldn't guarantee his spot if we waited; but there is no one on the waiting list at the moment, so that's a good sign."

"That's very kind of you, Nellie, really." Guilt washed over Sydney at the possibility that the only option to watch her friend's son could be taken away if she accepted the generous offer. "I don't want to abuse your hospitality, though. I'd already thought if I'm not better in another week, I should find a job of some sort. Then I could get a room in town somewhere and still help you out when you need to run errands. I really don't want to keep mooching off you and Nicholas."

"But you're not mooching, Sydney," Nicholas interjected.

"No, you most certainly are not. You're helping me so much with the house and the baby and with my sanity," Nellie said, laughing softly, "that I ought to be giving you more than just room and board. I ought to be paying you, like I'm willing to do." Nellie's temporary bouts of sadness had diminished a great deal with another adult in the house, especially one that had become a good friend.

"You're sweet, Nellie—both of you are—and I appreciate it." Sydney switched positions. Her legs were falling asleep crunched under her knees. "When exactly do you return to work?"

"My extended maternity leave is actually up Thursday, but I've asked to come back next Monday. The other nurses have been overly understanding, given my history." She smiled. "I work with a bunch of great women. It's almost like a family, the way they look out for one another."

Sydney was glad to hear Nellie had support outside of Nicholas. She'd explained her widow status and the hardships she'd had to go through since Ken's death. It broke her heart to hear such a story.

"Okay, well, I tell you what. I go back to Dr. Mitchell in the morning. If he clears me from his service and if I still don't have much more of my memory yet, I'll take you up on your offer *until* I can find a job. Hopefully, I'll be able to find something quick and simple within a few days *before* you start back. I'd rather not chance you losing Walker's spot; but if I can't find a job, I'll stay. Is that okay?"

"Not really. I'd prefer you to just stay with us and not worry about finding a job just yet. But if that's what you're offering and if it means you'll still be around town, I guess it'll have to do. At least Walker and I will still get to see you." She shook her head. "I'm sorry. Does that come across sounding like I hope your memory doesn't return? That's not what I meant. You've just become a very good friend, and I'd hate to see you leave here. I pray your memory comes back, and I selfishly pray you'll want to stay in Jennings."

Sydney put her hand on Nellie's arm. "You've become a good friend, as well. I understand what you are saying, Nellie, completely."

While Nellie nursed Walker in the truck, Nicholas cleaned up the remnants of the picnic. He placed the food back in the coolers and threw the paper products in a trash bag, tucked inside the basket. Sydney stood to stretch her legs. The sky was clear, keeping the clouds at a distance. Its rich, blue color dominated the expanse. The sun shone bright, warming her enough to take off her heels. Grass tickled the bottoms of her feet. A brown thrasher flew by, sharing its melody with creation. Sydney lifted her head and closed her eyes, letting the gentle heat from the sun energize her.

Nicholas finished packing away the leftovers and watched her as she stood a few feet away. She was quiet, deep in thought. A single tear slid down her cheek, glistening in the sunlight. He walked to her side.

"Hey, there."

She shied away, wiping the tear with her finger. "Hey yourself."

"You okay?"

"Just thinking, letting my imagination get the best of me."

Nicholas bent to pick up a blade of grass. "And what, pray tell, are you imagining?" he asked.

"What it'd be like to have a brother or sister."

"They can be a pain sometimes," he teased.

Sydney smiled weakly. "Maybe, but you'd be stuck with someone. You'd be connected to them for life."

"True."

"They'd be the one person who shared your past, your childhood. They'd know what you were like as a kid and when you grew out of those awkward stages. They'd know what it felt like when your parents acted so crazy, they embarrassed you beyond belief."

"True again." He rotated the blade of grass between his fingers, smiling to himself. "My sister and I were the only ones who felt the blood rush to our faces when Dad drove us to school in a broken van. And it was middle school, no less. Dad covered a back window that had busted out for some reason with a large piece of plastic and held it on with silver duct tape. He pulled into the school parking lot as a corner of that plastic flapped in the wind. What made it worse was the worn fan belt, screeching loud enough to be heard three blocks away. The sound yelled, 'Look at me.' We thought we'd be branded for life as *those* kids." He chuckled, trying to lighten the mood. "We learned, though, that as kids, all our parents do something at one time or another to embarrass us. We just had to hold out long enough for the next kid's parents to replace our story. Then that kid was labeled, and we were back to being Nelsons."

Sydney grinned, trying to picture what that day was like for Nicholas and Nellie. "That's a great story, Nicholas."

"Yeah, I guess it is. I've got plenty more where that came from. I'm sure your parents embarrassed you at one time or another, too." He paused. "You up for a short walk?"

"Sure."

They walked slowly, taking in the beautiful afternoon. A few small, white clouds rolled in. They were like cotton balls against a baby blue backdrop.

"Why are you wondering about a sibling relationship? Curiosity or did something come to mind?"

"Both, I guess," she sighed. "I'm just dreading that I'm an only child. It's only a feeling, but it's like all the other times when something starts to come back to me. It starts as a gut emotion and evolves into a vague recollection. The idea that I grew up without someone to tease or experience those moments with makes me—I don't know—a little sad, I guess. That's where the curiosity comes in. I want to know what I missed out on."

"It's not always fun and games, Syd. We had our good times, and we had our bad times. Every family dynamic is different, and every family experiences the good and the bad." He threw down the blade of grass and put his hands in his pockets.

"Your family would've been the same. Being an only child may be different than growing up with a sibling, but I'm sure you have your own stories. I'm sure you still have funny stories of your parents embarrassing you or vacations where one of you did something idiotic or tried something out of the ordinary. I'm sure you fought, and you made up—just like any of us. You have your stories, Sydney, and they are special to you and to your family, just like Nellie and I have ours. But that doesn't make them any less important or noteworthy."

"I know you're right. I just wish I could think of one . . . one to call my own." She looked down at her bare feet.

"You will. The stories aren't going anywhere. They can't be changed. Just give yourself some time. You'll find your way back to them, if God wills it. And whether He does or He doesn't, for some unknown reason, you'll have new ones. You'll have the story of the time you met a grizzly in the woods who turned into a prince charming." Nicholas elbowed Sydney in the arm.

"And what a story!" She laughed. Sydney felt herself relax. The man who had found her in the woods was good for her morale. They stopped for a second, so he could take off his shoes and socks as well. Apparently, the look of Sydney's bare feet was too much of a temptation.

"Better?" she asked.

He let out a sigh of contentment. "Ooh, yeah. Great idea." They continued walking, Nicholas holding his shoes by their heels.

"So, Nicholas Nelson, I'm curious about something else."

"Yes, Sydney Lost Girl, what might that be?" he gleamed with one eye raised.

She dismissed the tease, knowing he was doing it out of kindness. "Your dad's name is Nick; your name is Nicholas; and your sister's name is Nellie. What is your mom's name?"

"Patricia." Sydney couldn't help the laugh that escaped. "What's so funny?"

"I'm sorry. I just wasn't expecting that." He looked somewhat bewildered. "I just knew you were going to say 'Nancy' or 'Nichole' or 'Natalie'—some other name beginning with the letter N."

Nicholas relaxed his features and grinned. "Awe, the whole 'why are you all named with N words' question."

"Well? You've got to admit, it's a legitimate question." She looked up at him, interested in his answer.

"Truth?"

"Of course."

"Our mother never wanted to be called 'Mom.' And it would've been just weird and bad manners to call her 'Patricia,' so she came up with an alternative. She decided she wanted to be known as 'Nan' by her children and 'Nannie' by her grandchildren."

"Why?"

"She felt the title 'Mom' was aging. She's the materialistic type, always worried about the latest fashion and what she looks like. She considered mothers to be old and boring, with no fashion sense whatsoever." Nicholas paused a second as he thought about the handful of teachers at his school who were fashionable mothers. "She also wanted to find a name that could be used the rest of her life. She could be called 'Nan' and still feel young and by the time grandchildren came around, 'Nannie' would be a smooth transition."

Sydney thought about what he said. "Does she not see 'Nannie' as an aging name?"

"That's just it. She feels like we've called her 'Nan' for so long, that 'Nannie' is a term of endearment. Even though the rest of the world associates the name with a grandmother, ultimately meaning an aging woman."

She chuckled. "She sounds like an interesting character. I'd like to meet her one day."

"And so you shall, as soon as she returns from her girls' retreat," he said and grinned slightly. "Anyway, that's what led to the 'N' names. After I was born and named, my parents thought, 'We've got two down, why not keep it up?'"

"Well, I think it's a neat connection to family," Sydney commented, feeling, once again, the loss of her own family.

"Nick! Nicholas!" shouted Nellie. They turned to look in her direction. Her hands were cupped around her mouth. "Nick, Sydney, come on!" She waved, frantically.

"Wonder what that's all about?" asked Sydney.

"Hurry!" Nellie yelled in a shriek of panic.

"Something's not right. C'mon." Nicholas took off in a sprint, followed closely by Sydney. He dumped his shoes in one of the coolers before grabbing them and the basket, while Sydney scooped up her heels from under the tree.

"What is it, Nel? What's the matter?" asked her brother, almost shaking.

Nellie's chin quivered. "It's Dad. He's had a heart attack."

CHAPTER FIVE

Monday, April 11

2:00 a.m.

Sydney peered out the window of Nellie's guest room, feeling helpless. At two in the morning, the moon and stars remained hidden behind invisible clouds. Everything was dark. Everything was quiet. She felt like she was back in the woods, lost again without a clue of what to do. She had no idea what the morning light would bring, but she knew it'd be filled with emotions—this time, for those she'd come to care about.

She yawned, blinking away the water in her eyes. She was beyond tired. However, unlike her night in the woods, sleep refused to come. Her mind raced with uncertainties. Normally, her occupied thoughts rambled over her own reservations. Now, they were for what lay ahead for her friends.

Without their knowledge, Nicholas and Nellie's father had come home a day early from visiting his brother, while their mother remained with her college buddies on their annual trip to the beach. Yesterday afternoon, a neighbor had stopped by to bring Mr. Nelson his mail, as he'd been asked to hold it in their absence. Seeing the man's rental car in the driveway, he looked through one of the front windows of the house when there was no answer at the door. There on the floor, at the base of the stairs, he saw Mr. Nelson lying on the ground, unresponsive.

Fifteen minutes later, the man was en route to the hospital. He'd had a pretty severe heart attack, and his prognosis did not look good. The neighbor had immediately called Nellie's cell phone, and Sydney, Nellie, and Nicholas arrived at the hospital not long after their father. Nicholas had called Vincent on the way, asking him to meet them there. He was an hour away, in a neighboring town, but he said he'd be there as soon as he could. He'd been instructed to take Sydney and Walker back to Nellie's and return to the hospital with bags of clothes and other necessities.

Vincent had walked into the waiting room wearing several emotions on his expression. He'd looked angry, confused, frustrated, and deeply saddened. He'd seemed to have more on his mind than just the fact that his best friend's father was in the hospital. Whatever weighed on him, he kept it to himself. The hospital wasn't the time or place to discuss anything other than the present situation.

Nellie had handed her son to Sydney, kissing him gently on the forehead. She'd wiped away a tear that had fallen on his nose. Thankfully, she'd already started weaning him, so he'd be okay away from her for a while. However, not having Walker near her—her one constant—made her heart sink further. Nicholas had put his arm around his sister, smiled a weak *thanks* at Sydney, and then swapped keys with Vincent. Walker's car seat was in Nicholas' truck, and it was easier and faster to switch vehicles than to move the baby seat. Vincent wouldn't have minded moving the seat, but he didn't argue the point. It wasn't important.

Sydney left with Vincent and the baby, silently praying for the whole Nelson family and wishing she could somehow take the pain away. The drive to Nellie's was silent. They had nothing to say as they were both filled with multiple thoughts—sadness and unease and fear—all for their friends. The next day wouldn't be the day they'd expected. Nicholas wouldn't return to the classroom after a weeklong break, and Nellie wouldn't wake to the cooings of her son over the baby monitor while mentally preparing herself for work's return. It would hold something different.

Sydney had put Walker in his playpen in the den and went to pack a bag for Nellie. She'd found a few articles of clothing, her toiletries, and her Bible. She'd also thrown in a handful of snacks and bottled waters, enough for both her and her brother. Vincent nodded his thanks and left with the bag, still without a word. It felt like they were already at the man's funeral—everyone afraid to speak or not knowing exactly what to say.

He'd then headed to Nicholas' house to fill a similar bag of his belongings. He'd bring the siblings their bags and would more than likely stay the night with them in the hospital waiting room. He'd grown up with them. It was likely he felt Mr. Nelson was a father of sorts to him as well.

Lord, comfort them—all of them. Comfort Nellie and Nicholas especially. Guide the doctors' hands as they work on Mr. Nelson. Stand in the operating room with their father and in the waiting room with them, as well as on the trip home with Mrs. Nelson. If it's Your will, please heal him. And selfishly, Lord, stay here with me, too. The memory of Mom's death is still pretty fresh, and the thought of my friends possibly losing their parent makes me feel everything I remember feeling the day I lost mine. It hurts. Forgive my selfishness.

Sydney moved from the window and lay back down, trying once again to find sleep. She turned on her side, pulling her legs into a fetal position. Tears escaped her eyes, flowing quickly and quietly. She cried for her friends. She cried for their unknown. She cried for their father. She cried for herself, for her memory loss and selfishness. She cried for the confusion she felt, the confusion that could so clearly be intended to strengthen her if she could just learn to trust God with it. She cried hard and long, until she fell asleep from the emotional exhaustion.

6:07 a.m.

"Hello?" Sydney rubbed the sleep from her eyes. She looked at the clock. It glowed 6:07 a.m.

"I'm sorry to wake you, Sydney." It was Nellie. Her voice was barely audible from what, Sydney guessed, was a sleepless and trying night.

"Oh, not a problem." She sat up, hoping the elevated position would clear her grogginess enough to talk to her friend. "How are you? How's your dad?"

She heard a deep sigh through the phone. "He survived surgery, but he hasn't come around yet. The doctor said the whole ordeal was pretty bad, and if Daddy doesn't come to within a day or two . . ." Her words trailed off as she began to cry. Sydney sat quietly for several seconds.

"I'm so very sorry, Nellie. I'm praying for all of you. Is there anything I can do? Anything at all?"

Nellie sniffed. "No, not right now. In a little bit, I'll need to figure out how to see Walker; but for now, I just want to know how he is. I've never spent this much time away from him, and it's almost as hard as the reason I'm here."

Sydney tried to sound as upbeat as possible on four hours of sleep. "Well, he's great. You've done a wonderful job with him, Nellie. I had no trouble getting him to sleep, and I haven't heard anything from him since about one-thirty."

"Oh, good. Thank you." A small bit of relief tainted her sorrowful voice. Having to worry about her baby while worrying about her father was almost too much to bear. She felt strengthened knowing one worry was taken care of.

"For now, you can feed him the formula that's in the pantry. And the bottles are in the cabinet with the glasses. He doesn't like to take one, but he will if you're patient with him."

"Sure thing." Sydney heard the goodbye in her friend's words. She was done, having talked all she could. "Call me if you need anything."

"I will."

She was up now; and coming from the sounds through the monitor, so was Walker. The telephone must have woken him. He wasn't crying yet, though, so Sydney took advantage of his calmness and spent a few minutes trying to fully wake herself. Four hours of sleep would be hard to overcome. She quickly dialed Dr. Mitchell's office, leaving a message explaining she'd need to reschedule her follow-up appointment, took a hurried shower, and dressed for the day. Going on what the weather'd been like lately, she put on a pair of jeans and a red t-shirt. She wrapped a light jacket around her waist, knowing she'd probably need it if she visited the Nelsons at the hospital. It'd been cool in the building the night before.

She changed, dressed, and fed the baby before she had her first cup of coffee. Once he'd been taken care of, she saw to her own breakfast, which consisted of a couple pieces of toast and a banana. Walker played quietly in his playpen, while Sydney quickly inhaled her food. At five minutes after seven o'clock, she heard a knock at the door.

"Morning, Vincent. Any news?" she asked as she opened the door.

"Good morning." He stepped in, walking toward the kitchen with shoulders slumped. He looked about as well as she felt. Neither one of them had gotten enough sleep.

"He survived the surgery. But it doesn't look too promising." He poured himself a cup of coffee. The coffee maker was set on a timer to go off each morning at six-fifteen.

"Yeah, I heard. Nellie actually called about an hour ago. So I guess nothing new has developed." It wasn't a question, but an observation. "How are Nellie and Nicholas, actually?" She could only guess how they were by how she sounded. Vincent had seen them. He'd have a better understanding of their true demeanor.

"Uh, they're hanging in there for the moment—Nick a little better than Nellie. We all got a couple hours of sleep, which will hopefully be enough to get through the day." He stood against the counter, slowly sipping the hot beverage as he tried drawing energy from the caffeine. "Nan will be here this afternoon. Her friends didn't think it wise for her to drive so they booked her a flight."

Whatever mixture of expressions showed on Vincent's face the night before had disappeared. His long night had replaced the mixture with just one—concern.

"That's good. I'm glad her friends thought that through. A plane will get her here faster anyway." Sydney sat down at the table.

"Yeah," he said halfheartedly.

Sydney looked around the kitchen trying to think of something to say to ease the awkwardness that seemed to follow Vincent.

"If I'm still absent *me* by the end of the week, I'd planned on looking for a job, before Nellie has to go back to work. I don't want to intrude on her little family any more than I already have." She took off her glasses and rubbed the bridge of her nose. "Do you have any suggestions?"

Vincent put down his mug, his attitude solemn, but tense. "Yeah, as a matter of fact, I do."

"Great, what is it?"

"There's a novelty shop next to the grocery store in town. My aunt and uncle own it. They were telling me the other day that they could use a little extra help. My cousin's the only one who helps out, but he's off at college. They were hoping to find someone who wouldn't mind stepping in instead." He poured himself another cup of coffee, barely taking a moment's pause. "It wouldn't be hard—just sitting there mainly, minding the store. Every once in a while, a customer comes in; and you might sell something. But it's usually pretty slow. If you'd like, I could put in a good word for you."

Vincent felt he owed Sydney the help. He'd been walking on egg-shells around her, which sometimes came across as rude.

It was the longest speech Vincent had given, and she found herself smiling, feeling somewhat hopeful in the middle of all the chaos. "That sounds perfect. Yes, if you don't mind, I'd appreciate you talking to your aunt and uncle. And please, tell them I'm ready to work as soon as possible, as soon as Nellie doesn't need me anymore. I feel I owe her first billing. But hopefully, between myself and Kelsey, we can work out a schedule to give Nellie the help she desires."

Vincent nodded. It felt . . . right, doing something kind for someone else, though he didn't let the feeling linger. There was an underlying issue he knew he needed to address.

"What can I do? For Nellie and Nicholas?" Sydney asked, returning to the desperate situation at hand.

He shrugged. "I don't know. My guess is to continue looking after the baby."

"Absolutely. But is there anything else they need?"

"They haven't mentioned anything."

Sydney furrowed her brow. Why had Vincent shown up if there wasn't something else she could do, if he wasn't bringing instructions from the Nelsons? His mood swings bounced back and forth, sending her already-chaotic mind deeper into confusion. Sometimes, it felt like she was communicating with a brick wall. She never knew what to say or how to make him talk. One minute, he was quiet with little to say; the next, he was frustrated or angry; and then, suddenly, he was comfortable and ready for normal conversation. She'd never met someone so perplexing. At least, she didn't think she had.

Hospital

7:20 a.m.

"Daddy, can you hear me? It's me, Nellie."

Nellie sat in the chair next to her father's bed. The sounds of the machines beeped and pumped. It was an eerie, unsettling surrounding. Nellie's father was a big man, tough to the core, inside and out. In the CCU, he looked weak. Tubes extended from all parts of his body. His face was ashen-gray, life seemingly draining from his features. He lay there, quiet and still. Arms that normally never stopped moving were outstretched and motionless. A shiver went down her back. The strange sight of her father was foreign and heartbreaking.

Mr. Nick Nelson didn't have the greatest relationship with his two children. He loved them, and they loved him; but there was always something missing, a connection he couldn't make. Nicholas and Nellie shared a bond that he didn't understand. They claimed God was the reason they were so close. They'd tried talking to him, explaining what was so special about Him and His Son, Jesus. As much as he'd like to have a deeper relationship with his children, he couldn't, in good conscience, pretend to agree with something he didn't. He prided himself on honesty. A story of a God without a beginning or an end, Who created the entire universe—including man and animals—Who could part seas or bring on a worldwide flood, Who knew the number of grains of sand on a beach, Who named every star was a little too hard to imagine.

Even if he could accept a creation originating that way or those so-called miracles, accepting that a perfect God would send His Son in the flesh to this horrid, vile-filled place made no sense whatsoever. What kind of God would do that? What kind of Father would send His Son away to a place that was so harsh and unforgiving when the safety of His own home was available? What kind of Father would turn His back and willingly allow His Son to be killed? He was a father, and he would never even think about doing something so heartless to his children, even if they did have their problems. How could he agree to serve a God like that?

Nick could possibly be convinced of an existence of a Heaven and a Hell—that much he was willing to consider. But in his mind, Heaven was reserved for the Mother Theresas of the world. His idea of a Heaven was a slimly populated one. Since that didn't seem likely either, he chose not to put too much stock in the God of his children's fantasy. His own philosophy was that once you died, you stayed in the ground—body and soul. His lack of belief was as strong as his refusal to listen to what Nicholas and Nellie had to say on the subject. It was easiest on all parties if the topic just didn't come up.

Nellie leaned over to kiss her father on the forehead and whispered, "Be with him, Lord. I don't have the words right now, and You said the Holy Spirit will intercede for me. I'm trusting that. Thank You." She let out a shaky breath, trying to control her emotions.

Nicholas waited for her in the harshly lit area by the elevators. "How is he?"

"No change." He wrapped his arm around her shoulders as he pressed the down button. "I'm worried, Nick."

"I know, sis; so am I."

"He's showing no signs of improvement."

"No," he agreed, "but he's showing no signs of getting worse either. It's like he's plateaued."

She looked up at her brother through her quiet tears, a small smile pulling on the corners of her mouth. "I guess that's something, huh? 'No news is good news' kind of thing?"

"Exactly." They stepped in after the doors opened. The ride to the first floor was a short one. Nicholas silently prayed for his family and for wisdom in the many delicate situations that were sure to come. The elevator stopped as the ding upon arrival interrupted his prayer. They slowly made their way down the hallway, toward the cafeteria. "Nan called when you were in the back."

"How'd she sound?"

"You know her—has an outer layer thicker than a whale's."

Nellie chuckled through her sniffs. "She sure does, doesn't she?" A group of nurses bustled by, chatting too quietly to make out what they were saying. "One of these days, that outer layer is going to shed, and we'll finally get a glimpse of just how vulnerable Nan really is."

"I've seen it, though not often," Nicholas quietly recalled. "Sometimes, I've wondered if even Dad knows the real Nan." He reached into his pocket and pulled out a tissue, handing it to his sister.

"Thanks," she said. "Will she still be here by two?"

"It'll be closer to three. Said her plane's takeoff was delayed."

The food court was painted a pale gray, a usual color for a hospital. The somewhat-neutral shade didn't send out a cheerful message, but it wasn't gloomy either. A couple of nationally chained restaurants sat off to the left, opposite of the hospital's cafeteria.

"So, little sister," he said, sweeping his arm wide in front of them, "what do you want to eat? Omelet burrito, fried chicken biscuit, or whatever the special is for today?"

"Um, let's try the special. Hopefully, they'll have some homemade chocolate cake, too."

"For breakfast?" he asked, teasing. "Good choice."

Nellie's House

7:20 a.m.

"Vincent, is there something you *need*? I don't mean to be rude, but I'm a little baffled as to why you'd leave your best friend right now at a time of need and come by here so early in the morning if Nicholas or Nellie hadn't asked you to—if they didn't want me to do something, especially after I just talked to her."

He took a long gulp of his coffee. Sydney was surprised the liquid hadn't burned him on the way down. He placed the mug in the sink and leaned toward the window facing the backyard. His palms rested on the rim of the sink as he stared blankly outside. She glanced at his hands. They slowly turned white at the knuckles. He was beginning to make her uncomfortable.

She took a deep breath and asked again, slowly, "Vincent? Can I do something for *you*?"

He tilted his head back in disgust and twisted to face her. "Sydney, I've got something to tell you. Something you're not going to like. Something pretty bad."

She gasped. "Oh, no. I thought you said Mr. Nelson was hanging on?"

He shook his head. "No, it's not about him or Nellie or Nick." His breathing quickened just a bit. "It's about you."

"Me?"

"And me."

Sydney pushed her chair away from the table, stretching her legs. "I don't understand."

"Sydney," he exhaled, "we've met before."

"We have?"

"Well, I guess *met* isn't the technical term for it."

Her eyes squinted, bringing her brow inward and causing wrinkles to appear. "I still don't understand."

"I saw you the night before Nick and I found you in the woods. I saw you at a store about an hour from here."

"I'm confused," she said, staring at him questionably. "Why didn't you say something before?"

He moved the hair out of his eyes as he hesitantly strained to look directly at her. "What I'm about to say will likely upset you, as it should.

I wish I could explain why I did what I did, but I can't. I was a coward not to tell you earlier, and I'm sorry."

She motioned for him to wait a minute as she walked into the den to check on the baby. She had a feeling the conversation might take a while and would need to not be interrupted. Walker was content, playing happily with his teething toys. She returned to the kitchen, taking her seat again.

God, whatever I'm about to hear, help me.

She placed her hands on the table, folding them, ready to listen. He cleared his throat.

"Sydney, I was doing something at that store that I should never have done. I was with someone—someone I know to be inappropriate company. But I was there nonetheless. We were attempting to make a trade in the electronics section of the store. You were there, too—watching us."

Her mouth dropped. "I was spying? Actually spying? Like a stalker?"

Vincent quickly shook his head. "No, not at all. You're a good person now, Sydney, from what I can gather; and I'm pretty sure you were a good person then, too." He paused briefly, forcing himself to come clean. "You were looking at some cameras. You were far enough away from us that you shouldn't have been able to see anything . . . to be able to tell what we were doing. But you glanced through the camera's lens, testing it out. You caught us . . . making a drug exchange."

He willed himself to look at the woman, to study her expression as she listened to him. Her brow furrowed more intensely than before as her eyes narrowed in disbelief, and then suddenly in understandable horror as something registered.

A vision of the bag she packed for Nellie the night before flashed through Sydney's mind. It was green, just like the book bag Vincent and his partner used to put the drugs in. She looked up. His eyes. She'd seen those eyes before. She'd seen that face, that lanky figure. Unbelievable fear came over her. She panicked, looking around the room for something, anything that could be used as a weapon. She grabbed the butter knife she'd used for her breakfast toast. It sat idle on the table. She stood quickly, her chair shooting to the side. *Walker!* She ran through the foyer to the den and swiftly picked up the baby while simultaneously pointing the knife toward the man that had followed her.

A look of relief crossed Vincent's face.

"You remember, don't you?"

"Yes!" she yelled, panic stricken. "You killed someone!" She waved the knife wildly, trying not to let it slip from her shaky grip.

He held up his hands in an attempt to calm her. "We did, yes, but it was an accident. We didn't mean to hurt him."

"He was just a kid!" The words flew out of her mouth at an alarming speed. Some people may find fear puts things in slow motion. She was finding out the opposite. The adrenaline suddenly running through her veins shocked her system into overdrive.

"I know, Sydney. Believe me, I know." For the first time since coming to Jennings, Georgia, she heard pure calmness in Vincent's voice. Even his composure was relaxed. He was the complete reverse of herself. He opened his mouth to speak again, but she cut him off.

"Get out! Get away from me!" Walker began crying at the change in her voice.

"I will, but I wanted to tell you how sorry I was first. I should've come clean with you the morning we found you."

She blinked back tears forming forcefully out of fear. "Why didn't you? 'Cause your best friend was with you? You had to wait until we were alone?" Fright cracked through her words.

His shoulders slumped, though he kept his hands up to show her he meant no harm. "I told you. I was a coward. That's my only excuse."

"Who *are* you? Does Nicholas know the real you or . . . or is he . . . just like you?" She felt the gut-wrenching twist that thought brought.

"No, he's nothing like me. He's a good man. What you see is what you get with him." He tried to take a step forward; but she flinched, so he stopped. "I *am* Vincent Cobb, Nick's best friend. Down deep, I'm still the person he and Nellie grew up with. I made a decision—a decision to do some things differently—not long after Nellie's husband died. I didn't know what else to do." His eyes dropped as he ran both his hands through his sandy hair. "No, Sydney," Vincent said softly, "Nick and Nellie do not know this about me."

She couldn't process it all. She remembered everything. She remembered her name, her past. She remembered her family, her friends, her school. She remembered that night in the woods. She even remembered how she got there. It was information and emotion overload. Her head began to ache. It all flowed together, intertwining in a way that resembled a disoriented spider and its web. She couldn't grasp what was going on, what was happening at that moment. Why was he telling her any of it? Why now? Because she was alone? No one would come to her rescue if she screamed. She felt trapped. The walls around her moved inward, making it hard for her to breathe.

She glanced in the direction of the house phone. It was to her left, about ten feet away. If she kept him talking, distracted, she might have a chance to ease over there unnoticed. But once she had the phone, how would she dial the police without him snatching it from her?

Vincent followed Sydney's gaze as it met the phone on the end table behind the couch.

"Go ahead, Sydney. Call them," he said, calmly. "In fact, I insist." Relief continued to cover him, tainting his voice and his demeanor.

"I will," she stammered. "But I want you out of here first!" She didn't trust him to keep his distance while her hands were full with the baby, the butter knife, and the telephone. Her first priority had to be Walker's safety.

An idea formed as she looked at her two possible exits. Vincent blocked the front door, but the back door might be a viable option. She was closest to the dinning room, which connected the den and kitchen. She could dart through those rooms, grabbing the phone as she passed. The back door was on the other side of the kitchen. If she could make it outside, hopefully a neighbor would be out walking her dog or picking up the morning paper from his driveway. Getting herself out in the open was crucial.

"That's fair," he responded, slowly.

Her eyes found his, suddenly confused at another option. What was he saying?

"Syd . . . I really am sorry, so very sorry." He sighed, turning toward the front door, his back to her. "Just so you know, that accident was called in."

He closed the door and left. Sydney hurried to lock it, her hand frozen on the knob until she heard his vehicle drive off.

Vincent drove away from Nellie's house without the weight he'd been carrying on his shoulders for days. He'd finally told Sydney the truth. She'd reacted the way he'd anticipated, and he felt sure she'd call the police the minute he was clear of the house. That was fine with him. He was ready for everything to be out in the open, all the cards on the table. He didn't want to hide anything anymore. If they were ready to end this, he wouldn't put up an argument—not now. He was tired of the whole ordeal this path had taken him down.

Telling Sydney the truth brought about the result he'd wanted. She'd regained her memory. He'd hoped something he said would trigger it, and it did. She caught on faster than he'd anticipated, however. What was it that caused the chain of reaction? Whatever it was, he was grateful. He needed her to remember. He needed her to know what Zeke looked like. Vincent never had any intention of hurting Sydney, but he wasn't so sure about Roland's runner. If he found her, he might not be so forgiving. It was important for her to recognize him if he came into her inner circle. She needed that warning. She needed a warning about Roland, too, but the fact that Roland had never seen her was on her side. Vincent would warn Sydney about the man if—and only if—Zeke identified her. If that happened, Roland was sure to find out.

God, help us if he does.

"Jennings County Police Department, how may I direct your call?"

"Help me! I need an officer! Now! Hurry!" She grabbed her arm, steadying her nerves. Her hands shook uncontrollably.

"Okay, ma'am. Where are you?"

"Nellie Yates' house. Hurry, please!"

"Okay. I'm sending an officer your way. Is someone with you right now? Are you in immediate danger?" the dispatcher asked quickly.

"Yes . . . maybe . . . I don't know. I don't know where he went."

"Is he somewhere inside the house?"

"N—" She pulled in her lower lip, biting hard enough to draw blood. "No. Just drove off. But he could come back! Please! I need to talk to an officer!"

"He's gone. That's good. Try to calm down for just a second."

Calm down? How?

"What's your name?" The dispatcher asked, slowly this time.

Her name. Finally, she knew her name. She stammered, "Charlotte Hallaway."

"Good. Now what's going on, Charlotte?"

She exhaled to regain her thoughts. It worked. Words spilled out in one breath.

"I'm the woman who lost her memory. It's back now, and I need to report a crime. Happened Sunday, a week ago, at a superstore an hour from here. It involves Vincent Cobb." She knew the woman would make the connection. It was a small town, after all.

"Yes, ma'am. Stay on the line. I'll connect you with the detective looking into that case." She paused. "Just a moment."

That case? What does that mean? They know about it already? Must have made local news—suspicious death in a nearby store.

Charlotte peeked at Walker. As soon as had Vincent left, she'd put him back in the playpen and given him his pacifier. He'd continued to whimper for a minute or two, but eventually settled down and fell asleep. He looked peaceful, the complete opposite of how she felt.

"Mrs. Hallaway?" a baritone voice asked on the other end.

"Ms. Hallaway, Charlotte."

"Charlotte, I'm Detective Tom Jones. What can I do for you this morning?"

"Can you send someone over to Nellie Yates' immediately? I'm afraid I might be in danger."

"Already en route. Should be at your location in ten minutes." There was a long pause. "In the meantime, are you able to stay on the line?"

"Yes, he's gone . . . for now."

"Who is?"

"Vincent Cobb. Do you know him?"

"I do, yes," he answered. "What do you know, Charlotte?"

She began to pace, trying to compose herself enough to retell the story. "Late Wednesday night, my bus stopped in Greenes County really late. More like early Thursday morning. We were given a thirty-minute break because the driver had to refuel. I went into the store across the parking lot to pick up some film for my camera. While I was there, I saw a drug deal go down between Vincent Cobb and some other man in the electronics department. They spotted me and knew they'd been caught. They threw the drugs into a book bag."

She took a deep breath. Her blood began to boil. Anger would be just as potent as her fear in a few minutes.

"A young employee came up behind them. They didn't see him, and I really don't think he knew what they were doing, but . . . " She shook her head. "That doesn't matter now. The other man with Vincent stood quickly and slung the book bag and hit the kid in the process. He lost his balance and fell backwards. Detective Jones?"

"Yes."

"The boy hit his head. Blood. There was so much blood. He's dead." Charlotte bit her lip. This was real. How? She'd actually seen, first-hand, an unnatural death, a murder—a horrific, terrifying, never-leave-you kind of death. "I don't know what happened next because I ran. Vincent and his partner looked . . . angry. They knew I'd seen everything. I didn't know what else to do, so I hid until I felt like they were gone."

"I see."

"I would've reported it sooner, but I was in an accident right afterwards and lost my memory until just a few minutes ago."

"Was the accident related to the situation you just described?"

"No," she said, "I've probably seen too many made-for-TV crime movies, but . . . I was afraid they'd figure out who I was by somehow connecting my identity to the bus's passenger list. So I snuck onto a different bus. There were several at the bus terminal at that hour. All of those passengers were either out stretching their legs or asleep. No one saw me get on. I hid in the back of the bus, in the bathroom. I stayed out of sight, even when the bus left. I had no idea if Vincent and his partner were following me, but I wasn't going to chance it.

"After about an hour, we hit something in the road; and when the driver tried to regain control by overcompensating the wheels, we tipped over. I hit my head as the right side of the bus slammed into the asphalt. I managed to get off the bus, but I kept moving. I was still afraid the two men would find me."

Charlotte felt the tears slide down her cheek. The incident was less than a week old; but because of her memory's sudden return, it felt like it had happened five minutes ago.

"I guess I just froze. I was so concentrated on being invisible that I subconsciously made the decision not to tell anyone. I didn't even stick around to make sure everyone was okay." Her heart sank at the admission. She'd always thought herself a compassionate woman. Now, under extreme stress, she knew she fell short. *Forgive me for that, Lord.*

"Oddly enough, I was found by Vincent and Nicholas Nelson the next morning in the woods and miles away from the accident, without a memory and without identification. I had enough sense to grab my purse when the bus crashed, but I must've lost it somewhere between the accident and the woods."

"And how did your memory return?" the man questioned after a moment's silence, giving himself time to write a few notes.

What did that matter? She'd called him to discuss Vincent's crime, not her lack of memory. "I'm staying with a friend. Vincent just stopped by a few minutes ago and admitted to what he did. Something he mentioned at the beginning of his confession triggered it. It was like a domino effect. I remembered that incident and then suddenly remembered everything else."

"Does anyone else know about your memory returning?" asked the detective.

Charlotte let out a breath of frustration. "No. My memory just returned. As soon as Vincent was out of the house, I called you, no one else."

"So, I can take that to mean you haven't spoken to anyone else about what Dr. Cobb admitted to either, not even the friend you are staying with?"

"No."

"Is your friend with you now? Could she have possibly overheard the conversation between yourself and Dr. Cobb?" He sounded overly calm. She assumed that was normal, that he was just doing his job, collecting as many facts as he could. His calmness, though, did nothing for her own nerves.

"No, she's at the hospital. Her father had a heart attack yesterday, and she's been there ever since."

"I'm sorry to hear that." He cleared his throat. "Ma'am, I'd like to speak to you in person. The officer I've sent should be there any minute. I need for you to ride back with him to the precinct. Is that possible?"

"Detective Jones, are you going to arrest Vincent?" she pleaded.

"I'll answer any question you may have as soon as you get here."

Before Charlotte could argue, there was a knock at the front door. She instinctively jumped and then settled as she peered through the blinds to see the officer.

"He's here."

8:15 a.m.

Charlotte hung up the phone, opened the door to the officer, and collected Walker and what he'd need for an hour. At the precinct, she was directed to an interview room, which also served as a break room. Detective Jones fixed them both a cup of coffee.

"Charlotte, before I answer your earlier question of whether or not I'm going to arrest anyone, let me ask you a few." He paused, scanning a small notepad. "Did you get a good look at the man who was with Dr. Cobb?"

Without hesitation, she answered, "Yes."

"Good. That's very good. Do you think you could identify him if you saw him again?"

"Yes, I'm sure I can."

"Great. And would you be willing to testify in court about what you saw that night?"

"Of course. Should I look through some mug shots or something?" Charlotte was ready for this to be over. She rocked the car seat on the floor, keeping Nellie's son content. The baby didn't seem to mind all the noise from the police station.

"No, ma'am, that won't be necessary at the moment. We've been following the two of them for quite awhile now. I just need to know that we'll have an eyewitness when the time comes."

Charlotte slumped in the metal chair, the blood draining from her face. "When the time comes? Are you not planning on arresting them now?"

"Charlotte, before I continue, could you tell me what your occupation is?"

"My occupation?" This was getting ridiculous. What did her occupation have to do with Vincent Cobb and his criminal partner?

"Yes." Detective Jones answered with a steady ease, no matter how Charlotte's questions were asked. She was a ball of nerves; and for the life of her, she couldn't figure out the direction of the interrogation.

"I'm not working," she let out slowly. "I was in the middle of spring semester in grad school when my father died a couple of weeks ago. I'd been living with him; and after he passed, I decided to take a few months off and continue with my studies in the fall."

"I am sorry for your loss," he responded. "That does however, answer my question of your availability for the time being."

The room went quiet as the detective thought over his next possible move, sending shivers down Charlotte's back.

"Charlotte, I'm going to ask a huge favor of you. And if it's not something you feel comfortable with, you just say the word; and you can go back home, or we can put you in protective custody until this whole thing blows over." Her heart raced as beads of sweat formed on her brow. "You think you could keep all this to yourself for the time being and continue your day-to-day for the next week or two, as if nothing has happened? You think you could be in the same room as Vincent Cobb, without letting on to the others that something was said between the two of you?"

She stiffened, feeling the loss of blood in her face return in full force. Anger filled her voice. "Why would I do that? They killed someone!"

Detective Jones replied softly. "Yes, ma'am. Someone has died, and eventually the guilty party will be arrested for manslaughter."

"Eventually! Why not now?"

"There's another man in all this, a boss—the dealer. We have an idea of who he is; but right now, he's untouchable. I'd like to continue to follow these two in hopes of catching the bigger fish. You understand?"

"Not really."

The detective exhaled loudly and leaned forward in close to Charlotte in an effort to calm her before he spoke again.

"We need your help, Charlotte. We need help drawing this big fish out of the water. And we need time to do it."

Her mouth opened. "You want to use *me* as bait?"

"In a way, yes. This boss doesn't even know about you at the moment or about the failed drug exchange. But I'd feel better about the situation if you were kept in our jurisdiction for a little while longer. We're really hoping to nab this guy pretty soon."

"Do I have a choice?" Pinpricks to her head accompanied each word in the question.

"Of course, you do. We're not forcing you to stay—just asking. We can keep a better eye on you in our neck of the woods."

Charlotte put her hand over her forehead. Her headache escalated the more the man talked. A nightmarish detective television show was being played out, and she was the main character. She took a deep breath, trying to take in his words, to make sense of them.

"But . . . how can you guarantee my safety if I agree to stay?" She began to wish she'd never opened the door for Vincent that morning—that her memory had never returned.

"Honestly," he spoke carefully, "I can't. I can't *totally* guarantee your safety. We'll keep eyes on you—your comings and goings—and keep in constant communication. And aside from us, you'll also be around Vincent, since you already have some sort of connection or relationship with him. He admitted to what happened and then left you alone. Someone who does that is not out to intentionally harm anyone. I can tell you that I have complete confidence in Dr. Cobb and know he is not a threat . . . but that is *all* I can tell you."

The detective sounded sure of that point and like he was trying to convince Charlotte of its truth. He continued, "I'm not concerned with Dr. Cobb's conduct toward you. If I'm uncertain about anyone, it's the other man and, especially, the boss we're trying to catch. This mastermind, so to speak, has caused havoc for years. Frankly," he paused, "we believe he is dangerous and has had his hand in more than a few crimes, unreported officially. We've been after him for quite a while but have never had enough evidence to put him away for good. We don't have solid proof, but we're close. If we make an arrest too soon, it'd just be one man's word against another's."

Charlotte's eyes blinked in disbelief. It was too much to comprehend. She lived a quiet life. She ran from scary controversies and iffy situations. Now, she was smack dab in the middle of a major one. And she was being asked to willingly stay in that center.

"Have you seen the other man Dr. Cobb was with again, other than that night in the store?"

She ran her hand up and down her thigh, rubbing sweat off her palm. "No."

"Okay, Charlotte," he responded gently. "So, what do you say? We're closer than we've ever been to wrapping this mess up. Are you willing to stay? Just for a week or two? Do you think you can do it, pretend ignorance and be near Dr. Cobb without panicking? We don't want you to keep an eye out for anything unusual. That's our job. We just want you to get up every morning and go about your day, nothing different than what you've already been doing. If you can't, no one will blame you. We're asking a lot of you, and we'd understand if your answer is no."

Charlotte couldn't believe what was happening. She was a country girl who'd never experienced anything scarier than the top of a Ferris wheel at the annual fair. Could she be impartial around Vincent, with the visual of that crime now stuck in her mind? Could she relax enough so as not to draw suspicion? Could she keep going on as she had been, knowing what she knew?

What do I do, God? What do You want me to do?

Charlotte didn't know why or how the word came out of her mouth, but it did. "Yes."

"You sure?"

"I'll try," she answered shakily.

She could hear the relief in his voice. "Wonderful. Thank you. And Charlotte, if at any moment you change your mind or feel pressured or fearful, you call my number; and we'll immediately get you to a safe, private location."

He handed her a business card. Charlotte quickly stuck it in her pocket, deciding at that moment that she'd keep it on her at all times.

"One more thing?" She stood, her legs still somewhat shaky. "Do I need to keep the fact that my memory has returned to myself, or can I share that information with others?"

"I think it'd be best to tell them, but not how it came back. Dr. Cobb already knows your memory's returned; and since you're likely to be around him again, it stands to reason that your newfound memory will come up."

"And if he mentions what he told me to others? Or I get scared and change my mind?"

"Then we secure you here; or you can go home, and we'll explain the situation to law enforcement there. Don't worry. We'll be watching your whereabouts as well as theirs closely. Just remember, call if you need to, day or night."

Charlotte took a deep breath. Her life was changing, again. "Okay."

9:30 a.m.

Charlotte stood inside, watching the officer drive away after dropping her back at the house. Now that Vincent was away and the adrenaline to talk to the police had subsided, she felt more confused than she had the morning she realized her memory was gone.

Just a few days ago, she knew nothing. No one was familiar. Her mind was an empty shell. She didn't know where to go or what her next steps should be. She was ultimately facing each minute with one question after another. She had to depend on strangers to help her answer even the simplest questions. Now, her mind was full, filled with light instead of darkness. She knew everything. Everything, that is, except whom to trust. That realization was scarier to her than the unknown she'd faced over the last four days.

She wilted to the floor. Her head fell into her hands as she rocked back and forth on her knees. What had happened to her life? How had it gotten so out of control? Once again, she let out all her pent-up worries and uncertainties—this time, the new and old. She allowed herself to succumb to her emotions. She no longer had the strength she thought she had and was so proud of. No one was around to see her breakdown. No one would know of her weakness. Tears of confusion, fear, and sadness flowed from her eyes as she wept bitterly into her hands.

It was too much to take in, too much to handle. When her memory returned, *everything* came back to her. The good, the bad, the sad, the lonely, the happy—all of it came rushing through her at an alarming speed. All the emotions she'd ever felt dropped over her at one time, crushing her.

She couldn't compartmentalize it all. The thoughts and memories shot through her mind, bouncing from one side to another, passing other thoughts and memories doing the same. Her head was a pinball machine with hundreds of balls being released at the same time.

She was strangely and painfully aware of so many situations, situations that she relived like it was the first time they'd happened. She felt the death of her mother again, the loss of an older brother, the disappointment of a job that fell through, the ups and downs of relationships, and the despair of realizing she had no other family whom she could depend on after her father's passing.

She recalled vividly the decisions and actions that had brought her to Jennings, Georgia. She'd chosen to take a vacation, to get away for a few weeks. Her father, whom she loved more than life itself, had died from a massive stroke. She had no other relatives, none that were close enough to call family. She'd buried her father, packed a suitcase, called her intentions in to school, and got on the first bus leaving town.

It didn't matter where the bus was going, just that she was on it. Charlotte didn't want the hassle of driving. She didn't want to have to think about the other cars on the road or which exit to take. She just wanted to ride. She needed a change of scenery for a week or two. The bus she boarded was headed to Florida. The warmth and sunshine would be welcomed.

Remembering the death of her father was unlike that of her mother. It'd been years since her mother died. She missed her and mourned for her, of course. She had not forgotten her, but she had learned to live with her memory. God and time had done that. Her father's death was different. It was still fresh. She struggled to catch her breath at the thought of him. Sadness crushed her. She was a slave to the emotion. Her father, once again, rested in the forefront of her mind, still alive, not yet a memory.

Oh, God! What's happening to me? Why? Why are You taking me down this path? I don't have the time to work through Daddy's death because all of a sudden, I'm fearful for my own life. What do I do?

She heard James 1:5-6 from her heart as God whispered through her tears. *If any of you lacks wisdom, he should ask God, who gives generously to all without finding fault, and it will be given to him. But when he asks, he must believe and not doubt, because he who doubts is like a wave of the sea, blown and tossed by the wind.*

She let those words spread over her like a thick quilt, repeating the verses over and over. *Lord, I'm asking You for wisdom. I have no idea how I am going to walk into a room with Vincent Cobb and act normal. I have no idea how I'm going to be able to separate my emotions and fears, my regained memories, and the truth enough to function without others catching on. Please, show me what to do, and help me not to doubt.*

Charlotte remained on the floor, crying, until the sweet baby near her reminded her of his presence. She slowly lifted her head, peeking over the top of the playpen. Walker had already forgotten the tense mood that filled this house not but two hours ago. He cooed and happily moved his limbs back and forth. It was a baby's way, natural and predictable. The answer she'd been given was staring her in the face, in the motions of a three-month-old infant.

A trembling breath escaped her lungs. She would try her best to do what she knew to do, just like Walker cooed and moved because that's what he knew to do. When he learned something different, like rolling over or sitting up, he'd do that, too. But for now, he cooed. Yes, she would try to live today the way she'd been living until she learned something different, until God taught her something new. Her life was full of confusion. But God could use that confusion to teach her clarity.

Thank You, God, for the simple motions of a precious child. Help me to trust You to lead and direct my motions daily, hourly.

The telephone rang. Charlotte wiped the tears from her face. She'd been visibly upset for half an hour, though she'd reached her limit and was starting to settle. She steadied herself and answered slowly. "Hello?"

"Hey, Sydney, how's my baby? He wake up happy?" Nellie sounded tired; but even so, her voice was a soothing balm for Charlotte. She hoped she could be the same for her friend. The last thing Nellie needed was to catch on to her houseguest's distraught emotions.

Charlotte looked down at Walker and found her smile again, faint as it was. "He's just fine, Nellie. And yes, he did. He's definitely more of a morning person than I am. I gave him a bottle earlier, and he's already taken a short nap."

Nellie relaxed, sounding grateful. "Oh, good. I'm glad to know he's not suffering from my absence. Thank you, Sydney."

"How's your dad?" Charlotte straightened. She'd do her best to sound upbeat for her friend. Nellie depended on her.

"He's holding on, but barely."

"Oh, Nellie, I'm so sorry."

Nellie exhaled through the phone. "Me, too. There's not really anything we can do but to trust God. He's in His hands."

Charlotte could hear her friend's sniffling. She sounded more tired with each word spoken. "What can I do?"

"Actually, I was hoping you'd bring Walker to me. I need to spend some time with him. I'm thinking it'll do me some good. Plus, there's a girl here that I haven't seen in years, working as an x-ray tech. We were best friends back in high school. I passed her in the hall and told her all about Walker. He was the only topic I could talk about at the time, without erupting into a blubbering mess." Nellie's voice broke. "Anyway, she wants to meet him. I won't bring him inside the hospital.

I'll just sit with him outside for a while. There's a quiet little area with a peaceful gazebo behind the hospital."

Nellie needed recharging. Charlotte didn't blame her for wanting her son for that. If she'd had a child, she'd probably feel the same way.

"Sure, I'd be happy to. How do I get him to you? Vincent . . ." She tensed saying his name. " . . . Drove Nicholas' truck last night and dropped me off. I don't have a vehicle or a car seat."

"Nick said it was in the garage. Supposedly, Vincent and his uncle drove over there not too long ago to leave it with you. The keys are probably on top of the back left tire. That's where he and Nick always put them when they go hunting." She paused. "I figured he'd park the truck and leave since it was so early. Or did he actually stay long enough to speak?"

Charlotte's body tightened. She wasn't even going to have two hours to process what had happened to her or wonder how much she'd have to be around Vincent Cobb. His name had already come up.

One day at a time. Just live today, right, God?

"He did speak." She exhaled. "But he didn't tell me he'd brought the truck."

"Oh. You okay to drive?"

"I'm fine. I'll be there as soon as I can. Is there anything else you want me to bring?" Charlotte asked.

"Uh, yeah, my phone charger. It's by the bathroom sink in my room. Other than that, just bring me my new friend, Sydney, and my precious son." Nellie's faint smile could be heard through the phone.

"Absolutely!"

The phone call disconnected. Charlotte looked out the back door window into the garage. Sure enough, Nicholas' truck was there.

Charlotte quickly found the phone charger and a few other things Nellie might decide she wanted like magazines, a box of tissues, and a light jacket. She also grabbed Nellie's pillow and the blanket that was laid across the rocking chair.

She packed Walker's diaper bag with his necessities. There were enough diapers and changes of clothes to last a while, in case Nellie wanted him to stay with her longer. She grabbed a couple of clean bottles and the container of formula and placed them in a separate bag. Charlotte wanted to make sure everything was at their disposal. One never knew what one would need or want at a time like this. She patted her jeans' front pocket, making sure the detective's number could be felt. It offered a sense of security just knowing it was there.

The keys were exactly where Nellie said they'd be. Charlotte buckled Walker into his car seat and got into the vehicle. A note was taped to the steering wheel. She immediately locked the doors, panicking, and looked behind her. Walker sat playing with a toy. She peeled off the note and opened it.

I am sorry, Sydney, truly sorry. I should've told you immediately that I recognized you and who I was. I hope you will forgive me. Please know that you can trust me. I know that may be hard to believe right now. In time, I pray you will.

Sincerely,

Vincent

Her hands trembled as she reread the note several times, trying to read between the lines, and gracelessly refolded it. She slid the note in her back pocket. If she left it in the truck, Nicholas or someone else was likely to find it. That'd lead to the secret she'd agreed to keep, for the time being.

She slowly turned on the ignition, reminding herself of what Detective Jones had said. Vincent wouldn't hurt her because if he'd wanted to, he wouldn't have left her to call the police. He would've stopped her, somehow. But he didn't. In fact, he'd encouraged her to call them. That realization and the apology note sent mixed signals to Charlotte. She was more confused than ever.

10:45 a.m.

"You think that girl, the one with the memory loss, will be interested in the job?" the man asked.

"I don't know, Uncle Bob. I mentioned it to her, but I'm not so sure she'll be around much longer." Vincent stopped in front of his uncle's house. Bob Crane was a kindhearted man, always looking out for an underdog. When he heard about the woman with the missing memory, he wanted so much to help, but didn't know how.

"She'd mentioned earlier she may want a job until her memory came back, so I suggested she might try you and Aunt Gladys. She seemed interested at first; but by the time I left, she wasn't so sure."

"Oh, okay." Bob sounded a little disappointed. He reached for the handle. "Well, thanks for the late breakfast. It was nice catching up with my favorite nephew." Bob smiled, stepping out of the vehicle.

Vincent laughed. "I'm your only nephew, Uncle Bob."

"Even so, you're my favorite." Bob winked.

"I enjoyed catching up with you, too. We should do it more often. Thanks again for helping to get Nick's truck back to Nellie's."

"Any time."

"Tell Aunt Gladys I said hello."

Bob Crane waved his acknowledgment and headed inside his house. Though he and his wife had only one child, Vincent had spent so much time as a boy over at their house, playing with his cousin, it felt like it was his second home. Vincent was much more than a nephew or a cousin to them. He was loved like a son.

11:15 a.m.

Charlotte glanced in the rearview mirror, looking for someone in uniform. She reminded herself every few minutes that she was safe, that they were keeping an eye on her. She was being followed, even if there was no physical evidence of it. Not being able to actually see her protection was a true test of faith.

Nicholas stood in the parking lot of the hospital, waiting for her. The clothes Vincent had brought him had obviously not been used. He wore the same clothes he'd worn the day before. Charlotte thought how uncomfortable the church attire would've been during a hard, sleepless night in a hospital. His white dress shirt hung untucked and wrinkled. His tie, loosened. He'd obviously been too worried to think about taking it off. With head bent, hands stuffed in his pockets, and shoulders slumped inward, Nicholas appeared to be lost in thought. His usually upbeat attitude was downtrodden and unsure.

Charlotte slowed the truck to a stop beside Nicholas. She rolled down the window. It wasn't until she coughed that he looked up and noticed her.

"Oh, hi," he said, smiling faintly.

"Hey. Hope I didn't scare you."

"You didn't. I didn't even hear you." He pulled his right hand out of his pocket and pointed behind him. "Just pull in over there. I'll meet you and help with Walker."

"Okay." She rolled up the window and steered the truck into the parking spot. *God, calm me so that only You know my unsettled mind. Help me to be of service and comfort for this family. They've been so good to me.*

Though she should probably question Nicholas' motives and sincerity because of his association with Vincent, Charlotte didn't. Somehow, she knew that Nicholas was true to his character. After all, it'd never been him she'd questioned. Vincent was the one who'd always made her uneasy—he was the one who never seemed consistent in his behavior. Now, she knew why.

Walker was out of his car seat and into Charlotte's arms before Nicholas reached them. He looked into the back seat and grabbed the extra belongings Charlotte had brought. She saddened, seeing the bags under his eyes. They were dark and deep. She doubted he'd slept at all.

"You okay?" she asked, concerned.

He exhaled deeply. "Good as to be expected, I guess."

"Any change with your father since I talked to Nellie?"

"Not really. He's still there, but he's not. You know what I mean?"

A light breeze blew, sending chill bumps across Charlotte's arm. She ignored the small change in temperature.

"Yes, I do." She paused, thinking of any words that would offer encouragement. "The man you know is there, Nicholas. He's just going through something difficult. It may be changing his appearance and actions, but he's in there."

"I know." He shifted the bags from one arm to the other. "I haven't admitted it to my sister yet, but I struggle being in that room with him."

"What do you mean?"

"It just feels so . . . so final, for some reason. I almost don't know what to say. Funny, isn't it? Me, not able to find the right words." He let out a light chuckle.

Charlotte smiled. "It doesn't matter what you say. Just hearing your voice will be an encouragement. If you want to talk to him, talk to him, Nicholas. You talk all you want. He'll hear your voice, and I'm sure it'll bring him comfort. It'll be good for him whether you know what to say or not. Just talk. It'll be good for you, too."

They started walking. The gazebo where Nellie wanted to bring Walker was at a central location to the hospital. It had easy and equal access to all parts of the medical facility. An inner courtyard lay in the center of a circle of buildings. Each building was considered a wing or an extension off the hospital's main entrance. Nick Nelson was in Wing C. It was the cardiac wing. The gazebo sat to the northeast side of the courtyard.

"Maybe you're right," he said with a shrug. "I guess it couldn't hurt to try, huh?"

Charlotte nudged him with her elbow. "Nope. It couldn't hurt. And you never know, if he's the type of man who doesn't normally let you speak your mind, then you may think of something you've been trying to say to him for a long time. He can't stop you now. He can only listen. And hopefully, if it's important to you and if God allows, he'll not only listen, but he'll hear what it is you have to say."

She winked at Nicholas, returning a bit of his own past lightheartedness in an effort to strengthen him.

Nicholas stopped midstride. He looked at her, a revelation warming him like the sun breaking through clouds on a rainy day. She was right. He *could* talk to him. He could talk to his father, and his father could not walk out of the room. He couldn't put up a hand to cut him off. Nicholas had no idea if his father would hear him. He didn't know if he'd hear or understand anything he said, but it was worth a try. It was more than he'd been given in the past. It was an open window. Nicholas said a silent prayer of thanks and smiled, feeling hope for the first time when it came to his father.

Charlotte saw the sudden brightness in his sky blue eyes. "What? What is it?"

He started walking again with a new sense of optimism. "You're right. I can talk to him about something, and there's nothing he can do about it. I've had something eternally important to speak to him about for years. He's never wanted to listen. But now," he said with a gleam, "now I can and will speak about Jesus over and over. He can't hush me or leave. We can only pray Dad is coherent enough to comprehend it."

Nicholas looked at Charlotte, the bags under his eyes now not as defined. He had energy. He had direction. "Thanks, Syd. Thanks for your help. It's exactly what I needed to hear."

She was grateful he seemed more himself. "I'm just glad to see you smile again."

They found the gazebo. Spring surrounded it. Flowers were in full bloom. The trees and grass were a bright green, as everything in the courtyard spoke of new beginnings, of change for the better.

Another breeze rolled by. "Can you get Walker's blanket? I think it's in that bag." Charlotte pointed to the diaper bag in his right hand. Nicholas pulled out a blue, fleece blanket covered in yellow ducks. He wrapped it around his nephew, cuddled comfortably in Charlotte's arms.

"Thanks," she said. They sat on the white wooden bench inside the gazebo. "Nellie said she didn't want Walker inside the hospital. Do we need to get her, to tell her he's here?"

"She and her friend from high school will come out when they finish talking. Girls can get pretty chatty when they haven't seen each other for a while. I quickly volunteered to meet you when they got to discussing shopping and pedicures. Don't ask me why those were the topics when we are where we are. I guess that was their way of dealing." He leaned back, stretching his arms behind his head.

"Oh. Everyone has their own way, I guess."

Nicholas laughed. "What's your 'way of dealing'?"

She thought carefully over that question. "Well, let me see. I tend to deal with tough situations by running. Come to think of it, I tend to deal with any situation by running. The solitude and sweat seem to clear my head. I know most people are tired after a run. I get tired, for sure. But I also recharge. It helps me think clearly without distractions. Some of my best quiet times with God are while I'm pounding away on the pavement. It's like . . . " Charlotte considered. "I'm somewhere else. I feel myself melt inward. It's my closet, so to speak."

Nicholas looked surprised. "Sydney, I knew you remembered you like to run, but you're remembering something more, aren't you? That's *why* you like to run, not just that you like the exercise."

Even after a sleepless night and a scary personal experience, Nicholas Nelson saw something different about Charlotte. He read into what she said. He analyzed her answer and understood what was said without her actually saying it. She appreciated his insight.

"Sydney?" he asked again.

She struggled with herself. There'd been much more to her memory's return than she'd wanted. She desired so much to tell someone, to trust someone. Having someone else in this with her would be a supporting column. She thought back to her conversation with Detective Jones. He'd advised her not to confide in anyone about what she'd witnessed. Charlotte shook her head, willing herself to obey his suggestion, for the safety of her friends.

"Yes, Nicholas, I remember something more. I, um, remember everything, actually."

Nicholas bowed his head, a slow grin stretching across his face. Charlotte expected her friend to jump up and scream *yippee!* That was a reaction she imagined—he was an excited individual. Instead, he remained quiet, unmoving. He was happy; that much she could tell. But he was expressing that happiness in a way she'd not seen before. Several seconds passed. He seemed to be processing what she'd just shared.

He finally lifted his head and looked at her, relief filling his eyes. "I can't tell you how glad that makes me. It's so nice to hear something good after such a rough night." Charlotte switched Walker's position. His little body had begun to feel heavy. "So, I have two questions that come to mind immediately."

"Okay, shoot." Charlotte hated taking the attention from Nicholas' situation. However, if it brought encouragement to him, even for a moment, she was willing to endure the uncomfortable spotlight.

"What is your name?" he asked deliberately.

"Charlotte. Charlotte Hallaway."

"Charlotte, huh? I don't think that one came to mind when we were offering suggestions. Charlotte is a pretty name, though." He leaned back against the bench. "I've gotten so used to calling you Sydney, it may take me awhile to make the switch. You'll have to be patient with me."

Nicholas was a kind friend. The thought of him calling her by her given name actually sounded a little odd. He was used to calling her Sydney, and she'd gotten used to hearing it, even though it had been only for over half a week. The name was the first piece of individuality she'd been given when she was without a memory.

"You know," she said and smiled, "if you don't mind, I'd kind of like it if you'd continue to call me Sydney. It'll be my unique reminder of how we met, of how you and your sister took me under your wings and helped me through a difficult time. It'll be a reminder of how special your friendship is to me."

He grinned. "I'd like that. After all, you're a Sydney in my mind. The name Charlotte doesn't roll quite as well off the tongue."

She nodded. "And your second question?" Charlotte asked curiously.

"Um . . . " He hesitated. "Is there a husband or boyfriend somewhere that is on his way to Jennings, Georgia, to pick up his missing wife or fiancée?" He shifted uncomfortably.

Charlotte let out a burst of laughter. "That was subtle."

"Thank you. I try." He joined in her laughter for a quick moment and then asked again, anxious for her answer. "So?"

Charlotte kept the corners of her mouth tilted upward. It felt good to feel something positive after such morning brouhaha. "No, Nicholas, there is not a husband or boyfriend on his way."

He turned his head so that their eyes met. "Good."

12:45 p.m.

"Ooo, Walker, you are just precious and so big!" Nellie's friend lifted the infant high in the air, bringing a smile to his chubby face.

"That's what happens with babies, Hannah, when you meet them three months after they're born," Nicholas teased.

She brought Walker back down and cuddled him. "Oh, stop it, Nick. I had no idea Nellie and Ken had a baby. If I had, I would've made a beeline to this sweet thing." She pinched his cheek.

He lovingly slapped her across her shoulder, looking down at his nephew. "Yeah, yeah. No one said you had to become a high-class technician, working long hours and never seeing outside those white walls. You chose that path all on your own. You could've stayed and helped at the store with Mr. and Mrs. Crane. I recall them begging you to work for them summer after summer. Something to do with their son having a little crush?" He threw his head back in a boisterous laugh.

Hannah carefully withdrew one arm from underneath Walker's back and quickly sent a playful punch Nicholas' way. He anticipated her move and dodged the jab.

"Very funny! I guess I have been a little out of it lately. Actually, I've been overseas, taking a year to just travel and see the world."

"Really?" Nicholas asked, intrigued. "How did I miss that?"

She looked up from the baby. "It's called life, Nick," she responded, throwing a little back at him. "We went all over Europe, people watching and eating the coolest foods."

"We?"

"Two of my cousins and our mothers." Hannah bounced Walker in her arms, watching his eyes lighten in excitement.

Nellie cleared her throat, busting to talk. "Go on, Hannah, tell him. He was like your brother back in the day. He deserves a chance to check the guy out."

"Guy?" asked Nicholas, feeling the urge of protector rise.

Hannah Tatum had been a much-missed piece of Nellie's life when Ken died. For one reason or another, the two of them had parted ways years ago and hadn't reconnected until yesterday. They'd been each other's closest friend throughout middle and high school. Hannah had spent so much time at their house over the years that Nicholas felt he had two sisters to deal with at times. Hannah's brother was ten years younger than she was, so she depended on Nicholas—whether she realized it or not—to make brother-type wisdom calls when it came to the boys she dated or classmates that bullied her. Her lazy eye was often the butt of jokes in those middle grades, and Nicholas had stepped in more than once on her behalf.

"Yep, guy. I met a great one in Italy. He's an American from Texas and was on vacation with his family. We ran into each other and got to talking. Turns out we had a lot in common, so once we parted ways, we kept up communication through phone calls." Her hazel eyes beamed. "Long story short, months later, he proposed, and I accepted."

Nicholas smacked his hands together. "That's great, Hannah, really great. I'm assuming your parents approve? 'Cause if they don't, I'll need to meet this fellow before you tie the knot—check him out for myself."

"Yes, and they love him. It's all good, I promise."

"Okay, then. Well, congratulations. We're truly happy for you."

"Thanks." Hannah handed Walker back to his mother and released her smile. "So sorry about your dad. Nellie's been filling me in. That's a tough situation to go through."

"It is." Nicholas took a seat on the ground, his smile fading at the reminder.

Nellie bent to kiss her son's forehead, breathing in the tender love she needed to rejuvenate her own spirits. His sweet innocence brought a quiet calmness.

She then lifted her head, realizing she hadn't yet introduced her two friends. Pointing to Charlotte, she said, "Hannah, this is our new friend, Sydney. Sydney, this is our dear childhood friend, Hannah Tatum."

Charlotte had liked her immediately, liked the way they all interacted together, as if they were family. She stuck out her hand in greeting. "Hello, Hannah. It's very nice to meet you. And congratulations. That's exciting."

"Thanks. Nice to meet you, too." She reciprocated. "Nellie tells me you've been a huge help. I know she appreciates it."

"It's no problem. I'm happy to help anyway I can." Charlotte stepped back, taking a seat next to Nicholas on the small area of concrete slab under the gazebo. He squeezed her shoulder gently, thanking her in his own way for being a friend to himself and to his sister.

"Yes, I do!" said Nellie, as she and Hannah found the bench. "You really have been a huge help, Sydney."

"Actually," Nicholas interjected, "turns out we need to be thankful for Charlotte, not Sydney."

Nellie lifted her head curiously. "Who's Charlotte?"

Nicholas grinned, eyeing Charlotte. "Sydney?" asked Nellie. "You remembered your name?"

"Yeah, I did. Everything, really. It all came back a few hours ago."

Nellie nearly shouted in her excitement. If she hadn't been holding Walker, Charlotte felt sure she would've jumped for joy, embracing her in a delighted hug. "Oh, Sydney, that's wonderful! I'm so happy for you."

Her friend's reaction was what Charlotte had expected, unlike what she'd received from her brother. "Thanks, Nellie. It's a lot to process, but at least it's back."

Nellie smiled sympathetically. "So, Charlotte, huh?"

"Yep, that's me, Charlotte Hallaway. But you can keep calling me Sydney if you'd like. Nicholas is sticking with the name, and I'm good with it."

Walker's arm lifted, and Nellie rested her thumb in his palm as his fingers wrapped comfortably around it. "No, your name is Charlotte; and that's what I'll call you. Sydney can be Nick's pet name of sorts for you; but to everyone else, you will be who you are—Charlotte Hallaway."

Nellie let a single tear escape her eye. She was emotionally overwhelmed, experiencing despair over her father's situation to bliss for her new friend's recollection.

The early afternoon was pleasant and encouraging on many levels. Nicholas had been given an open window with his father that he planned to take later that day, if circumstances allowed. He'd gotten to see Charlotte, which always made him happy. Her memory had returned, and he'd found out she wasn't connected romantically to anyone, which meant he had an open window with her as well. Nellie was able to relax as she spent some much-needed time with her son, and Nicholas was able to take a short nap, finally falling asleep as they all sat outside, soaking up the sweet sunlight. Nicholas lay down on the grass and listened to the women converse quietly about anything that came to mind. Eventually, the low chatter pushed him into a peaceful slumber.

After some time, Nellie fed her son and asked her friend to take Walker back to the house. He was almost ready for his afternoon nap. Once Nicholas had escorted Charlotte and Walker back to his truck, he spent a few silent minutes with God, thanking Him for the return of Charlotte's memory, praying for the guidance in Hannah's upcoming marriage, and for the wisdom of all involved in his dad's situation. Then Nellie stepped back to visit her father, while Nicholas spoke with the doctors to see if there'd been any change. They assured him there hadn't.

3:15 p.m.

"How'd Nan sound when you talked to her between flights?"

"You know Nan," replied Nellie. "Cool and collective about everything. She calmly digested the most recent doctor's report and didn't let me know how it affected her."

"It affected her, Nel. Everything affects her, just like it would anyone else."

"I have no doubt, but . . . she has a funny way of not showing it, you know?"

Nellie wrapped her napkin around her late lunch. The airport pretzel was hot. "I know she's not, but sometimes she seems cold-hearted, like she doesn't know how to show sympathy. I'm used to it after all these years, but that doesn't mean I don't wish things were different."

Nicholas sighed and nodded his hesitant agreement. "It's her front, that's all."

Nicholas and Nellie met their mother at baggage claim. Patricia Nelson was a walking example of outward class. Although she'd just come from a vacation at the beach and had been told her husband was on his deathbed, she strolled through the airport wearing a smile, an orange-patterned sundress, a shear white sweater, and the latest fashion in sandals. Her hair had turned white prematurely for her satisfaction, but she wore it with pride in a short, elegant cut.

"My babies!" She opened her arms just wide enough to express her desire. Her children met her and simultaneously hugged her. "Where's Walker?"

Nicholas let go and grabbed the luggage off the spinning rack, while his sister clung to his mother. One always needed a mother's hug, even if that mother was Patricia Nelson.

"He's with a friend. I wanted to see you and visit with Dad one more time before going back to the house this evening. Since I stayed at the hospital last night, I think I'll go home and spend some time with Walker."

"Of course. I do hope I'll be able to see my grandson soon. I bet he's grown a foot these last two weeks," Patricia said as she let go of her daughter.

Nellie shrugged. She wasn't ready to be released from the embrace, but her mother apparently was. She couldn't remember a time when Nan had ever held her long enough to ease the hurt of life's circumstances. It was always an *I'm sorry, honey; now, it's time to get back out there* kind of hug. She prayed God would give her the compassion for her son that he'd need during those uncomfortable stages. Nellie never wanted Walker to feel lacking in that department.

"Not quite, but sometimes it seems that fast," she sighed.

Nicholas balanced two bags, one in each hand. "Is this it?"

"Yes, dear. Thank you."

Patricia looked at her son and daughter carefully, seeing neither had apparently slept much last night. Her heart sank. Her husband had had a heart attack alone and been found by a neighbor. There was no telling how long he'd lain there, waiting for someone to help. Her children had dealt with the sudden news of their father without her and without sleep. She'd not been there to soften the blow of his appearance, to explain what they'd see before they walked into the hospital room. They had to carry that burden alone.

She silently shook off her sadness and lifted her chin, showing the world she would get through this. They'd all get through this. After all, they were Nelsons. They'd take control, and the patriarch of the family would survive. Patricia Nelson was a determined woman and always got her way.

7:30 p.m.

Nellie walked through her front door too tired to think. She'd been up for the better part of thirty-six hours. She knew she should talk to Charlotte to find out if she was okay. Her memory had returned, and she knew she'd need a friend's listening ear. Nellie recognized that necessity, but with the emotional rollercoaster she was on and with no sleep, she honestly didn't think she could be that ear, not now. All she could focus on was getting to Walker for a few minutes and then crashing on her bed until morning.

"Charlotte?" Nellie called softly from the foyer. She didn't want to waste energy walking in one direction if Charlotte and her son were somewhere else.

"In the kitchen," Nellie heard and slowly began making her way to the back of the house.

Charlotte glanced at her friend as she came into view. She could tell she was standing only by sheer determination. It'd been a very long day and a half, and the evidence on her friend's face was convicting. She and Nellie had both met their limit, coming to its end from entirely different directions. A solid night's rest was what they both needed, and the sooner the better. It'd hopefully give them each a clear head and the energy they required to face whatever lay ahead.

Charlotte breathed in the last bit of drive she could find and spread a tired smile across her face. She'd need to be the stronger one for a while longer. She may be emotionally spent, having found her memory and suddenly fearful for her life, but Nellie was emotionally and physically drained. She had nowhere else to go but down, until the physical aspect could be altered.

"The neighbor that found your dad dropped supper off a while ago. I'll have the food in your room before you finish feeding Walker. He's already in his PJs and playing happily in his bouncy seat upstairs." The infant chose that moment to make a happy gurgling sound through the baby monitor. "If you'd like to talk about your father, I'm happy to listen. If not, you can catch me up tomorrow. After you've spent as much time with Walker as you'd like, I'll take the monitor with me and deal with anything that comes up during the night."

Nellie couldn't speak. She'd put all her concern into her father for his salvation and his health. She had worried over her family and her new friend's situation. She knew she needed to keep going, to give just a little bit more. But she was empty. She had nothing left to give. God had just answered a prayer she hadn't known to pray. He'd sent her a blessing. Charlotte wasn't asking her to give anymore. She was asking her to receive.

Nellie fell into the closest chair, all her limbs suddenly weak. She doubted she could lift a pencil. The bit of kindness Charlotte had shown her gave her permission to let it all go. She sobbed loudly and uncontrollably, too exhausted to be embarrassed. She wasn't the type to normally breakdown like this in front of others, not since Ken had died. But it felt good. It felt like something she had to do. The tears fell freely until her eyes began to hurt. She felt God's embrace as Charlotte Hallaway's arms wrapped around her shoulders.

Thank You, Lord, for sending me a friend in Christ. I had no idea I would need her, but You did.

Nellie never opened her mouth to thank her friend. She just didn't have the strength. Charlotte seemed to understand; and without words, the plan Charlotte had laid out was executed. Nellie rocked her son, drawing from his ignorance of the day. She fed him, kissed him on the forehead, and placed him in his crib. She handed the monitor over to Charlotte, as instructed, and went to her room, where she found her supper on a tray atop her bedside table with a note: *Come to me, all you who are weary and burdened, and I will give you rest—Matthew 11:28.*

Charlotte hadn't spoken either, not since Nellie began to cry. She said nothing, knowing that human words were not what she needed to hear. The verse was the first thing that came to mind when she saw how beaten down Nellie had become.

Nellie read the verse and smiled. *I am doing just that, Lord. I'm here with You. Please, give me rest.* She ate enough to stop the grumblings of her stomach and then fell asleep until morning.

CHAPTER SIX

Tuesday, April 12

9:00 a.m.

The women sat in the kitchen, eating their breakfasts of grits and eggs. Both had slept soundly, thanks to Walker doing the same.

"How's your mother?" asked Charlotte, rubbing her calf. *Cramp.* "Did she stay at the hospital last night?"

Nellie refilled their coffee mugs and handed Charlotte hers. "Nan is . . . oh, we all call her that, by the way."

Charlotte smiled. "Yeah, I know. Nicholas filled me in on the name origins. I think it's a neat story."

"I guess. I thought it was just plain weird when I realized all my friends called their mother 'Mom'; but now, it does come across as rather unique and special, in a way." Charlotte nodded her agreement. "Anyway, Nan is doing as well as to be expected. I don't know if Nick told you, but she puts on a pretty tough exterior. Everyone around her is convinced that she can handle anything. Truth is, Nick and I learned a long time ago that it's just a mask.

"One afternoon, we heard her crying in her room, when she thought no one was in the house, over something hurtful someone had said about an event she'd chaired." Nellie mixed her grits and eggs, adding a bit of salt. "I remember thinking how strange her crying was.

141

She always came across as hard and uncaring. Still does. She really makes it difficult to see that soft side.

"With Dad's heart attack, she's remaining strong for us; but she has to be breaking inside," continued Nellie. She swallowed a small bite. "I'm not exactly sure if she stayed at the hospital last night, but if I had to guess, she did. I left before she'd made her final decision."

Charlotte was just about to ask about Nicholas when a loud knock at the back door silenced her. She jumped, splashing the simmering coffee out of the mug in her hand. The hot liquid seared her fingers. Knowing what she knew, she doubted her nerves would calm down anytime soon.

Nellie patted her hand before reaching for the paper towels already on the table. "It's okay, Charlotte. I'm sure it's just Andy, Ken's brother. I called him to tell him about Dad, and he said he'd be by as soon as his plane landed. He's been so good to Walker and me since Ken died—a real help. Not sure what we'd do without him." She rose to unlock the door as Charlotte soaked up the spill.

A tall businessman entered the kitchen. He was over a head taller than his brother's wife and wore a sour expression mixed with fatigue. The plane ride must've been demanding. He quickly dropped his luggage on the floor and scooped Nellie up in an embrace. She allowed the hug, taking in a deep breath and silently wishing it was from her husband. Andy Yates smelled like Ken—a combination of laundry detergent, spearmint, and new car.

Both brothers had a soft spot for their deceased mother's favorite laundry detergent and gum, keeping her memory alive by refusing to give up those favorites. The new car smell was from all the rentals they rented for business trips if they weren't flying. For some reason, the aroma stuck in every business jacket, lingering for weeks. This scent was still just as intoxicating as it was a year ago when Ken died.

Andy and Ken travelled a lot, often for weeks at a time. Ken started out working with him, marketing the newest toy to would-be buyers. But after he realized how much time it'd take him away from Nellie, he chose to work from the office, allowing Andy to live the life in and out of hotels without him. It was a pay cut, but worth every dime, especially since his time with his new bride was shortened by a lifetime.

Ken had been an amazing husband. They'd met at one of the town's high school football games. Most of Jennings came out to support their boys, even if they personally didn't have one on the team. It was a whirlwind romance, something Nellie had never done. Normally, she took months to feel someone out, to know him well enough to form a decision to date or not. With Ken, it was different. They hit it off immediately. After only six weeks, she knew she'd marry the man. Four weeks after that, they were man and wife.

Their marriage was wonderful, just not long enough. He came home, showering her with adoration. At least twice a week, Nellie received a new bouquet of flowers at her door or a small trinket wrapped and hidden in her car or under her pillow. They were inseparable, always laughing and enjoying just being together. They went to the movies or out dancing in the nearest city or just stayed home, talking late into the night. Nellie was truly happy. But far too soon after they were married, Ken was killed in a car accident. His car was found in a ditch outside of town. According to the police report and the skid marks, he'd swerved to miss a deer.

"Thanks for coming, Andy. How was your trip?"

"Same as usual. Trying to convince clients to buy things they're not sure they want." He released his sister-in-law and stepped back, catching sight of his nephew in the bouncy seat. Andy bent down to pick him up.

His eyes flashed to the woman beside Walker, studying her intently as he asked almost out of necessity, "So, you must be Sydney, the woman without a memory?"

Nellie interjected as she walked to the cabinet to retrieve a plate for his breakfast. "Andy, this is Charlotte Hallaway. And yes," she added before he could question, "this is also Sydney. Her memory returned yesterday morning."

"Is that so?" he asked with a crooked grin.

"Thankfully, yes. It's very nice to meet you, Andy." She smiled as she nodded her greeting and dropped the coffee-soaked paper towels into the trashcan.

He returned her smile with a full set of perfectly straight, pearly white teeth before shifting the baby to the other arm. "It sounds as if you've been a big help to Nellie. And for that, I thank you. The idea of her going through something like this in this house alone is bothersome. I'm glad you were here." Andy spoke quietly, apparently tired from his journey.

"So, what's the latest with your dad?" he asked, turning his attention back to his sister-in-law.

Nellie put the plate of grits and eggs on the table, motioning for him to sit. "Nick called about forty-five minutes ago saying there was still no change." She hesitated. "The doctors have said if he doesn't show any sign of improvement today, they don't expect he ever will."

She absentmindedly poured him a cup of coffee and added cream and a spoon of sugar.

"Well, now that I'm here, I can watch Walker-man if you want to head back over to the hospital. He's taking a bottle every now and then, isn't he?"

"Yes, but not completely."

"Perfect. I'll bring him to you when you need him." Andy placed his nephew back in the bouncy seat and sat down to his breakfast.

Charlotte watched the whole scene unfold. Nellie's closeness to her husband's brother was obvious. She hadn't asked if Andy wanted something to eat or how he liked his coffee. He hadn't asked to be fed. It was assumed. There was a comfort between the two of them.

When Nellie explained that her father hadn't gotten any better, Andy's response was to volunteer to watch Walker instead of going with Nellie to the hospital. And in turn, essentially freeing Charlotte's time. It's possible he believed she could be more help to the Nelsons at the hospital. She suddenly shuddered at the thought. That scenario came with another consideration. Vincent Cobb.

Lord, I'm trusting You.

11:50 a.m.

Nicholas Nelson had called Charlotte asking if he could take her to lunch. His invitation had a two-fold purpose. He knew Andy was back in town and would be happy to stay with Nellie for a while and occupy Walker. Nellie was still pretty wiped and could use another solid hour or so of rest before coming back to the hospital. According to the medical staff, the afternoon and evening could be the hardest parts of the day. She'd need all the energy and strength she could get.

Nicholas also wanted to escape the stiffness of the waiting room himself for an hour or two while he learned what he could about the woman he'd found in the woods. He planned for them to eat in the hospital's cafeteria, so he could still be close if something went wrong with his father during his time away. Charlotte seemed more than willing to comply.

He opened the unlocked door to his sister's house, knocking as he did. "Hello? Anybody home?"

He could hear his nephew crying from upstairs. Charlotte stepped into the foyer from the kitchen. She looked beautiful and preoccupied.

She sighed heavily as she greeted him. "Hey, Nicholas. How's your dad? Any change?"

"Afraid not. I didn't get a chance yesterday; but this afternoon, I'm going to try to use his quietness to my advantage." She looked at him puzzled and then smiled gingerly as the meaning registered.

"I'll make sure I'm praying for you as you do." Charlotte grabbed the extra house key Nellie had given her, and they walked to the truck. He was still driving his father's F-150. He hadn't really had the time to switch the vehicles. Even if he did, he doubted he would. His father's truck was roomier and would be a better fit if he had to transport others to and from the hospital.

"It's appreciated." He opened the passenger side door for her. "I'm assuming Nellie knows you're going out?"

"Yeah, I told her I'd leave when you arrived. She's busy trying to calm Walker enough to leave him with Andy, so she could take a short nap. She said she'd meet you at the hospital in a while." Charlotte shook her head, still hearing the ringing of his wails in her ears. "That kid's been crying for the last twenty minutes."

Nicholas grinned. "He tends to fight sleep with a vengeance when he'd rather be doing something else."

"Don't we all," she replied, adjusting the vents away from her face. "I'm sorry you had to drive over here to get me."

"I had to grab something for Nan from their house anyway. You were on the way back." He leaned forward, booting the temperature up a couple of degrees for Charlotte. He usually liked his truck cold, often forgetting others didn't.

"Oh." She subconsciously looked in the passenger side mirror as Nicholas backed out of the driveway. "How is she today?"

He gritted his teeth, showing off his strong jawline. "Not so great," he admitted. "I mean, when you meet her, you'll think she's fine, not at all what you'd expect for someone with a spouse of almost forty years on his deathbed to behave. But to me, her lack of fidgety movements tells me she's in a lot of pain. Normally, she paces a room and talks to everyone. She's a people person and always likes to hear and share a good story.

"And," he paused to look for traffic before crossing an intersection. "She usually carries her planner with her everywhere. She jots down ideas for new events, corrections for past ones, and reasons some should be omitted altogether. Her mind never stops."

"And she's not doing those things?" Charlotte softly asked.

"No, she's not." He twisted, popping his back and leaned his head against the headrest. "She's hardly moving at all. It's like her energy level bottomed out. She sits in the chair and smiles politely, engaging in just enough conversation that others think she's fine. I've yet to see her jot down anything. In fact, that's why I went by their house. I decided she didn't have her planner with her."

"Ah," Charlotte concluded, "you thought getting it would make her as fine as she's pretending to be." She hesitated, praying for wisdom. "Nicholas, it's okay for her to not be okay. It's natural, what should be, in this situation."

"I know, and I'd be really bothered if she didn't show some kind of sadness. But at the same time, it's hard to watch—especially from someone who never shows anything but control." He pulled into the hospital's parking lot and brought the vehicle to a stop. His hands dropped to his lap in frustration. "I can't help Dad, Sydney. He's stuck in that room, covered in tubes and machines. He's helpless, and I can't do anything about it. But," he said with a sigh, "if there is something I can do for Nan, I need to do it. You understand?"

Charlotte reached over and put her hand over Nicholas'. "You were not made to fix everything, Nicholas. You're a good son. You pray for your parents, and you're there for them. That's all you have to do. Keep praying for them. Stand by them. That's what they both need—your prayers and the knowledge of your presence. Neither of them expects you to fix anything. That's God's job. Let Him do it, and let Him use you to be their supporting column."

12:15 p.m.

Nicholas took Charlotte to a seat in the far corner of the cafeteria lobby. It was crowded, as hospital staff and families of patients filed in for a quick bite to eat. At least the corner was secluded enough for a quiet, uninterrupted conversation. They'd each selected the homecooked menu of lasagna and a tossed salad, with banana pudding for dessert.

"So what do you think about Nellie's brother-in-law?" Nicholas smirked, reaching for a breadstick.

Charlotte hesitated. Andy Yates was polite, kind, and very attentive to Nellie; but she couldn't help noticing the look in his eyes as he'd first noticed her. She couldn't quite figure out its meaning. Had he paused to study her because he found her attractive, or was it because she was someone new in his sister-in-law's house?

"Um, well, I guess you could say the jury's still out."

He laughed, almost choking on his bread. "I really don't think anything else needs to be said. You're wise not to answer until you've had enough time to form your own opinion. He'll make that clear for you sooner or later."

Rather than respond to the possible indication he was a lady's man, she poured dressing over her salad. Nicholas grinned at her self-control.

"I want you to know, I've called my bank and cancelled my cards, since I lost my purse. I explained the situation with my memory and the weekend and asked if they could overnight a new one. More like begged. I'd like to hang out for a bit—with your dad in the hospital and all. I think they felt sorry for me," she said with a wink, "because they agreed. So when it arrives, I'll pay you back for Dr. Mitchell's bill. Nellie mentioned you covered it for me."

Nicholas looked at the woman he'd rescued and almost wanted to laugh. She'd had her memory back for a day, and already she was trying to pay back debts. Could she not enjoy finding herself for a few moments first?

"There's no hurry; and if I didn't think you'd argue with me until you got your way, I'd assure you there's also no need."

"Well, I'm glad to know you get that. I will argue, and I will win." She chuckled.

"Enough money talk," he said and grinned, taking a sip of tea. "Sydney/Charlotte Hallaway, if you're up for it, I have a list of questions I'd like to ask, now that you have your memory. It's been a rough couple of days in here, and I think it sure would be nice to get my mind off Dad and on someone much prettier—at least for an hour."

"I don't know what to say. Thanks? Or, no pressure, huh?"

"I was thinking, 'Sure, Nicholas. I'll answer anything you ask.'"

"Okay. Go for it. I'm game for a little while at least." Charlotte cocked her head, before adding, "Until I feel like you're getting out of hand." The hour away would be just as nice for her, keeping her mind off of her own scary situation.

"I'll take what I can get." Nicholas blessed their meal after swallowing the bite of bread. "Ready?" She nodded. "Question one: What's your middle name?"

"Ann. I was named after my great-grandmother."

"What is your favorite color?"

"Orange."

"Favorite season?"

"Fall. No contest."

"How about flowers? Which type do you prefer?" he asked, ready to make a mental note of her answer.

"Daisies. Probably not what you expected, huh?" She shrugged her shoulders. "They're not the most glamorous flower, but I think they're fun. I remember, as a girl, picking at the petals and pulling them off one by one saying, 'He loves me; he loves me not,' with each stripped petal. I used to sit in our backyard with a handful of freshly picked daisies. Each boy in my class got a flower. Johnny loves me. Johnny loves me not. Or Stan loves me. Stan loves me not. Whichever boy's flower ended with the last petal on 'he loves me' was my abstract boy-friend for the afternoon, until I did the whole routine again the next day." Charlotte chuckled, remembering how silly she'd been.

Nicholas just smiled. He enjoyed watching his date remember her past. He felt like he was being given a special glimpse as she relived those moments for the first time again.

He tore apart another bread stick. "Food and drink?"

"Hot dog and a tall glass of iced strawberry lemonade."

Nicholas grimaced. "Hot dog? Really?"

She laughed. "Yep, but I don't tend to admit that to too many people." Charlotte took a bite of lasagna as his expression lingered. She'd been told more times than she could count what was in a hot dog, so she'd learned to keep that bit of information about herself silent. The ingredients that made up a hot dog should've altered her opinion, but it didn't. She just ignored its origins and ate it, preferably grilled. Comfort food is always best from the grill.

"I don't blame you. I wouldn't either."

"So, what about you? What are your answers to all those questions?" she asked.

He tore open the small, papered-packaged pepper, adding it to his salad, and mixed in the dressing. "Oh, is that how it's going to be? Okay, I can work with it." He paused as if considering a question that needed more thought than what had been asked.

"Let's see . . . my middle name is James, after no one in particular. Nan just liked the name. My favorite color is red. I think flowers are pretty to look at, but I could care less about learning their types. I'm a meat and potato man, and my favorite season is also fall. I'd much rather the boys play soccer then. It's a definite difference in temperature."

Charlotte understood that. She greatly preferred to run in those months when the temperatures were beginning to drop and the leaves were changing.

Their banter continued in the same way until they'd learned most of the superficial things about each other. They found out each other's favorites in books, movies, sports, vacation spots, and music. It was a lighthearted meal, full of fun and laughter. They'd each relaxed enough to recharge their personal batteries. Both had pushed to the back, for the moment, the troubles that awaited them.

Nicholas knew he needed to get back upstairs to his family. He knew he needed to do everything he could to share Jesus with his father. He glanced at his watch. Visiting hours would be open again in twenty minutes. A sigh escaped. He had twenty more minutes to pretend things were okay—twenty more minutes to spend with Charlotte by himself, without having to be the strong one his mother and sister depended on.

He thought about leaving things as they were with his date, thought about the need to head upstairs, but he couldn't help himself. He wanted to know the superficial things as well as the deep-seated thoughts and events that defined this beautiful, freckle-faced woman in front of him.

He took a sip of his water, collecting the words in his head before he asked them. "Syd? Were you right about your inclination of being an only child?"

She finished her last bite of lunch and put her fork down. A look of sadness came over her as she placed her hands in her lap and leaned back against the metal chair.

"Yes and no," she said softly. Nicholas studied her as he waited patiently for her to explain. She pulled off her glasses and rubbed the bridge of her nose.

"No, I wasn't an only child the first eight years of my life. I had an older brother, Kyle, who teased and pestered me relentlessly—as only a sibling does—and who also loved and adored me when no one was looking. He was the only one allowed to pick on me, I guess you could say. If anyone else tried, he'd jump into protector mode until the kid stood down."

Charlotte smiled tenderly, recalling a particular memory of Kyle's face as he tried to shoo a tyrant first grader away with an attempt at an intimidating look.

"Kyle was a good brother, and I was blessed to have him as long as I did, although it took years to get to that point of thankfulness." She sighed.

"What happened?"

She kept her eyes on her empty plate. "He went hunting with some friends one weekend. Kyle didn't care too much for the sport. He didn't really want to go that day, but the other guys begged him. He was well-liked and so funny that people just wanted to be around him." She sat up straight, leaving her stare where it was.

"The guys split up into twos and headed to their desired hunting spot. His buddy'd already climbed the tree stand and was sitting on the small seat where they were going to hunt. He held out his hand, ready to receive the gun Kyle was trying to pass over before he sat next to him. Each boy thought the other had a solid grip on the gun. Neither actually did. The gun fell to the ground, unloading a shot that went straight through Kyle's heart. He died instantly."

Nicholas brought his chair around to Charlotte, pulling her hands from her lap. They were ice cold. He wasn't sure if it was because the lobby area was a little chilly or if the memory had caused it, but he wrapped her hands in his.

"Oh, Sydney. I'm so very sorry."

"Yeah, me, too." She breathed in heavily. "Ever since then, guns and hunting don't sit too well with me. He was only sixteen, but he was old enough to know not to load his gun until he was ready to shoot." She turned to look at her date.

"The first month, I was so mad at him for that. I remember yelling at his picture in his room, lecturing him, the way he used to do to me about not touching a hot stove or looking both ways before crossing a street. It seemed almost that simple, like it was common sense, a known fact to every hunter."

He continued to hold her hand, gently rubbing circles on the back with his thumb. "Kids are just as human as the rest of us, Syd. And teenagers, unfortunately, can make very stupid and dangerous mistakes. A lot don't think before they act. He didn't leave the bullet in the gun to prove a point or to be brave. He likely thought nothing could happen to him, as we all do at that age. Probably wasn't even thinking about safety. Checking the barrel before he left to go hunting that morning or even when he'd finished the last time was quite possibly just a passing thought. Considered one minute. Forgotten the next. It wasn't intentional."

Charlotte withdrew her hands so she could swipe away a tear that had escaped. "I know that now. Actually, I figured that out pretty soon after his death. But it didn't help my eight-year-old self process life without him. I went through all the emotions, but anger was the strongest until I learned to forgive Kyle's carelessness."

She sniffed and forced a slight smile. She'd said all she wanted to about her past. She needed this time with Nicholas to be carefree and stress-free. A week of what-ifs had passed, and a week of what could be was just beginning. An hour or so of "who cares" was what she wanted now.

"Okay, I think I'd like to call it quits on the get-to-know-you questions for today."

Nicholas gave her a quick side-shoulder hug and conceded. "Deal. Let's see . . . we could always talk about the weather." He winked. She tilted her head back and released a light laugh. Her friend was good at lifting the mood at a moment's notice. She enjoyed being in his company more and more each time they were together.

1:15 p.m.

"Yea, Roland. I saw her, saw her good. If I ever run into her again, I'll know it's her." Zeke ran his hand through his hair, second-guessing himself for telling his boss about the girl.

"You boys got sloppy! You never should have let her get away. If you had followed my orders, we wouldn't be in this situation. When I tell you to meet somewhere, I expect you to do exactly that!"

Zeke heard an angry grunt through the line. He should've kept his mouth shut. Vinnie told him to. He told him the girl probably didn't see them enough to make an ID. But it made him nervous, knowing there was someone out there who could be holding his one-way ticket to prison. If Vinnie wasn't going to help him track her down, Roland would. Or at least put the scare in that supplier, who'd gone too soft to do his job.

"And, Zeke," Roland growled, "You're going to pay for this—both of you—one way or another. And if the two of you ever make a mistake of this magnitude again . . . " The sentence trailed off as the call disconnected with an angry slam. Zeke was fully aware of what the consequence would be.

1:30 p.m.

Nicholas and Charlotte made their way upstairs to the cardiac floor after their cafeteria lunch date. He'd volunteered to take her back to his sister's, but Charlotte had asked to stick around, hoping against her better judgment to cross paths with Vincent. She'd agreed to stay in town for a while, and Detective Jones felt confident that Vincent wouldn't hurt her. Approaching him about the job he'd mentioned would hopefully ease her mind enough to trust the detective's beliefs. It gave her an in, something to discuss other than what she'd witnessed. She prayed that was the right tactic. Charlotte didn't dare come in contact with him alone, if she could help it—not yet anyway. At least if his best friend was with her, she'd feel a bit more secure when she saw Vincent again.

She was surprisingly calm as she stepped into the elevator. She took a deep breath and sent up a quick prayer.

Okay, God. Here goes. Give me strength to see this through and to do it in a way that somehow gives You glory.

Nicholas placed his hand on the small of her back and guided her onto the ICCU floor of Wing C. They walked quietly down the hall until they reached the waiting room. She stretched for his hand, silently drawing from his strength. He squeezed, as the corners of his mouth tilted up, keeping his eyes straight ahead at what awaited each of them.

Mr. Nelson's small group of loved ones took up a fourth of the waiting room. An elegant woman—whom Charlotte decided was Mrs. Nelson—Nellie, a middle-aged couple, and Vincent all looked up at the arrival of two more additions. Charlotte shuddered at the sight of the gangly man. Nicholas felt it and looked down at her, confused. He sent one final squeeze of reassurance and then released her hand.

"Anyone with Dad?" he asked, knowing visiting hours were no longer closed. Charlotte kept her eyes on anyone but Vincent.

"Not at the moment. They're changing his sheets." The woman stood and gave him a gentle hug and then peered over at Charlotte with interest. "And is this the young lady I've heard so much about from Nellie?"

Nicholas smiled. He placed his hand on her back again and began the introductions, pointing as he called a name. "Yes, this is Sydn—I mean, Charlotte Hallaway. You can all call her Charlotte, while I'll stick with Sydney, her chosen name during memory loss. And Sydney, this is my mother, Patricia Nelson, and Vincent's aunt and uncle, Bob and Gladys Crane, who are also very good friends of the family."

The older couple nodded. "It's very nice to meet you all," said Charlotte as casually as she could.

"Sounds like you've had quite the ordeal," Mrs. Nelson responded. "Nellie told us your memory had returned. That's wonderful news." Charlotte smiled in agreement as she took in the description of their mother for herself. She was a beautiful, elegant lady. Her words were cheerful and considerate, though Charlotte could tell they were forced. She'd been through the deaths of her own mother, father, and brother.

She understood fake conversation better than most and was probably the only one in the room who truly picked up on it.

Nicholas gestured toward his best friend. "Yeah, did you hear that, Vin? It all came back to her yesterday morning. Isn't that great? Now we can figure out why she was in the woods." He looked back at Charlotte. "I can't believe I didn't have that on my list of questions earlier." He leaned down and whispered, "That'll give me an excuse to ask you out again." He winked as she smiled unsurely.

Vincent cleared his throat and stared at his friend's object of affection. "Yeah, man. I did hear that. Actually, I was there when it came back." Charlotte jerked her head up and glared at him in complete confusion. Was he going to tell everyone here? Now? He kept his eyes on her as he spoke. "It was when I stopped by to give her your keys to the truck. Something I said must've triggered it. I could see it all come back as soon as it did."

"Really?" asked Nicholas curiously. He pulled her in for a quick hug of excitement. "What'd he say that brought it back, Syd?"

Charlotte couldn't release her eyes from Vincent's grip. What was he trying to do? He was clearly giving her a way out. She could rat him out, right now, in the middle of the ICCU waiting room in front of all these people. She'd be protected. Surely, he wouldn't try anything here. She cocked her head in concentration as her mind went another direction. Or, he was showing her that he was right. He could be trusted. Why else would he give her such an easy and clear way out of this mess if it wasn't to prove he meant what he said?

Is that really it, God? Can I really trust this man?

If Vincent Cobb really wasn't the bad guy in all this, then who was? His partner? The bigger fish Detective Jones had mentioned? She flashed back to that night in the superstore. It wasn't Vincent who'd killed the boy. But it was Vincent who'd admitted to what happened and then left her alone, unharmed. Why? What was his reasoning for telling her and then leaving her to call the police? Guilt? Was he really just a good guy caught up in a dangerous situation?

Charlotte blinked, keeping her eyes on Vincent. She was going to have to truly trust him, to accept the possibility of the truth behind his promise of not hurting her. If she didn't give in to that promise wholeheartedly, she'd be on edge for who knows how long. She liked Nicholas and Nellie and wanted to keep spending time with them. Vincent Cobb was close enough to be part of their family. He'd be around a lot. So if she wanted to know the Nelsons, she'd have to surrender to the felon.

She pulled her gaze from Vincent and glanced back up at Nicholas, pushing an unnatural smile. "Um, well, he was talking about a book bag, and I suddenly remembered a similar one from my past. Then it all came rushing back at once. Strange, huh?"

Charlotte turned back to look at him. His mouth had slightly opened. He looked surprised, very surprised. At that moment, she felt the tension leave her shoulders. No, she was no longer fearful of this man. If Vincent Cobb was that shocked that she chose not to take the out he offered, he would not hurt her. She trusted his intentions, as vague and confusing as they were.

Nicholas laughed. "Seriously, a book bag?"

Charlotte shrugged her shoulders. "Yep. Crazy, isn't it?"

"I'll say," Vincent mumbled as he slid his hands through his hair and leaned back in his chair, looking at the ceiling.

The group sat in the waiting room discussing Mr. Nelson's health, the latest professional baseball game, and whatever else came to mind that was considered small talk. Vincent watched Charlotte from his occupied corner chair. She nodded politely or responded to a question or just sat and listened to the conversation. She seemed calm. The transformation was unreal. He'd given her a wide-open door. All she had to do was walk through it, and his secret would've been out. Vincent couldn't figure out what had happened for her to accept him, for her to choose to keep quiet.

He wanted to talk to her in private. He had to know what she was thinking. But before he could formulate a plan of action, Charlotte had found her way to the empty chair beside him.

"Why?" he whispered as he rubbed his palms back and forth on his jeans. The hospital suddenly felt like a furnace.

Charlotte leaned forward, matching his position so only he could hear her. She folded her hands in her lap.

"I called the police after you left. The detective seemed to know about your case already and suggested there was a man in charge that was hard to find. He asked me to stick around. He tried convincing me that you were safe, that you wouldn't hurt me, and that knowing you might help catch the guy."

She paused, knowing full well she'd just told him more than she should've if she questioned his intentions at all. Her life was literally in his hands.

"I wasn't so sure until I realized that you didn't have to tell me in the first place, and you didn't have to walk out of Nellie's house yesterday on your own accord or encourage me to call the police. And then, just now . . . you clearly gave me another chance to expose you."

Vincent couldn't help but slap his knees out of irritation. Even that didn't deter her.

"Yes, I did! So, why on earth didn't you take it? I'm so tired, Sydney." He shook his head. "Or Charlotte, or whatever your name is. I'm tired of living this lie. I just want to start over, to say *no* this time. It's too much responsibility. In any other circumstance, I'd go to jail for this mess, but ... " He paused briefly, hoping that last comment would send her questioning mind into overdrive. It hadn't. She didn't even flinch. A frustrated sigh escaped his mouth as he absentmindedly popped his knuckles, then mumbled, "In all that explanation about the man in charge, did he even tell you the guy's name? Did he explain that part?"

"No."

Vincent quietly grunted. Charlotte had never heard the man sound so ... so normal. He wasn't discussing everyday topics, but his demeanor was consistent—aggravated, for sure, but consistent. He wasn't bouncing from one emotion to the next. He wasn't nervous or unsure of what to say. His conscience was clear, at least with her, and he was finally able to express his thoughts. Her heart actually went out to him. At that moment, she realized she had forgiven him. She felt free herself, still fearful of what the end might be with the other men involved, but free from the hold Vincent had had on her.

She reached over and took hold of the hand that was now resting on his knee. He quickly jerked it away and looked at her in complete surprise.

"Vincent," she said calmly, "I want you to know that I forgive you. I forgive you for keeping your knowledge of me to yourself for days. I forgive you for scaring me beyond words. But," she paused, "it's not up to me to forgive you for the crimes you've committed. You didn't commit them against me. You committed them against that superstore, the young boy who died and his family, and most importantly, to God."

Vincent began to shake. "Why?" he asked, shuddering. "I don't deserve it."

Charlotte smiled. "None of us do, Vincent. We've all sinned, and we've all fallen short of the glory of God. Your sin of being involved that day is no worse than mine of unjust thoughts. It may have far greater consequences for those around you; but in God's eyes, sin is sin. And the only punishment sin deserves is death." She let out a sound of sweet appreciation and contentment. "Aren't you glad Jesus took that punishment upon Himself? Otherwise, none of us would've ever made it out of infancy."

She tried taking his hand again. This time, he let her. "Vincent, if I can't forgive others who've sinned against me after what Jesus did for me on that cross, I'm not grateful for His sacrifice, for His willingness to forgive me. And that is one thing I don't ever want to be. I don't want to ever look at the cross and see just a piece of wood. I want and need to see the blood, to remember the blood that was shed on that wood. *Telling* Him thank you is not enough. I need to *live* thank you."

"Hey, guys," Nicholas interrupted. They both lifted their heads as Vincent cleared his throat, silently storing Charlotte's words for later. "Nel's going to sit with Dad, while I drive Nan home and let her take a shower. She wants to stay here again tonight, so they've put a cot in his room for her."

Nicholas looked down, noticing Charlotte's hand on Vincent's. He shook it off. Surely, his best friend wouldn't make a play on the girl he liked. "Vin, you mind giving Sydney a ride home if she's ready to go before I get back?" Nicholas peered over at Charlotte. "If you don't mind, of course."

She released Vincent's hand. "No, I don't mind." She stood, putting her arm through Nicholas' and directed him to the side. "Let me know how your talk with your father goes. I'll be praying for you."

"Thanks. And thanks for going with me today." He patted her hand. "I had a really nice time. You were just what the doctor ordered," he said with a wink.

"I had a good time, too. Promise to do it again soon?" she asked hopefully.

"Without a doubt." Whatever that was with her and Vincent, Nicholas didn't think much of it after that comment.

Nicholas and his mother said their goodbyes and made their way out of the cardiac ward. Charlotte glanced over at Mr. and Mrs. Crane. Now that she was on good standing with their nephew, she thought she'd mention the possible job opening they had. If all settled with Mr. Nelson, sitting alone at Nellie's with Nellie and Nicholas at work and Walker at daycare would get old pretty quickly. Worse, it would give her mind too much time to imagine. And honestly, should she even stay with Nellie anymore?

God, what if my staying with her puts her and the baby in danger? I don't want to be the cause for that. I know Detective Jones said just a week or two, but . . .

"Hi, Mr. Crane, Mrs. Crane." There were no empty seats near them, so she bent down next to Gladys Crane.

"Hello, Charlotte," the petite woman answered. "Please, do call us Bob and Gladys. Any other way makes us feel so old."

"Sure." She smiled, extending one leg to a more comfortable position. "May I ask you something?"

"Certainly," said the woman.

"Vincent mentioned to me earlier that you might possibly have a job opening at your store. If that's still the case, could I apply or interview for it? I'm looking for something local just for a few days. I know it won't be long, but I'm hoping to find something to pass the time while I'm here."

"But why don't you just go home, dear?"

"Well, I think I'd feel more comfortable sticking around a little longer. I'm trying to figure some stuff out about what I'm remembering. Plus, it probably wouldn't hurt to hang out for a while, in case my memory slips again for some reason. It may be better to be safe than sorry. Since Dr. Mitchell is the one who saw me initially, it stands to reason he'd be the best one to see me if I had a relapse."

Charlotte bit her lower lip, suddenly realizing she needed to reschedule her follow-up appointment. Maybe his bedside manners would improve once he knew her memory had returned. Somehow, she doubted it.

"Oh, I see." Gladys turned to look at her husband. He nodded in response to the silent question she asked. "Well, yes, dear. Sure you can have it."

Charlotte stood. "No, ma'am, you don't understand. I was asking to apply or to interview. I'll follow the proper procedures just like anyone else. No favors, please."

Bob chuckled, resting his arm across his wife's shoulder. "We aren't offering any favors. We just have no other applicants, and the job has been listed, by word only, for quite a while now."

Charlotte grinned. "Well, in that case, I'll take it. When would you like me to start?"

2:50 p.m.

Vincent drove Charlotte to Nellie's house thirty minutes after Nicholas left the hospital. They rode in silence. He was still processing what had just happened, and she was likely quiet for the same reason. The skies began to darken as rain clouds moved over Jennings. It was expected to rain for the next several hours.

He pulled into the driveway and slid the gear into PARK. Neither moved.

"How do you do that?" he asked.

Charlotte turned to look at him. "Do what?"

"*Live* thank you."

"I don't do a very good job of it, I'm sad to say. But I do try to keep the idea of it in my thoughts throughout the day." She picked up her purse from the floorboard and placed her hand on the door handle.

"I'm selfish, Vincent, and I'm human. I'm not perfect. Only Jesus is. I sin every day and have to ask forgiveness for those sins. To *live* thank you is a goal. Sometimes, it's a good day, and I can lay my head down at night knowing I've attempted to reach a part of that goal. Sometimes, it's a bad day, knowing my selfishness stepped in and I didn't even come close. But always, it's a failed day, because I'm a sinner and will always fall short.

"I try because I love Him and want to bring Him honor and praise, but I'm never enough on my own. It's only through Christ that I can even make an effort each day." She opened the door and smiled kindly. "When He calls me home to Heaven, I'll *live* thank you; I'll *sing* thank you; I'll *dance* thank you; I'll even *breathe* thank you. And I'll do it without an ounce of myself getting in the way. There's no sin in Heaven—just a whole lot of thanking and praising."

Charlotte stepped out of the vehicle, recalling the whole afternoon. It had been unforeseen, and she was still in awe at how it played out.

"Thanks for the ride, Vincent."

"You're welcome." Charlotte shut the door and walked toward the front of the house. Vincent rolled down his window and hollered, "Thanks for the forgiveness, Charlotte."

She peered over her shoulder as her expression softened even more. "You're welcome."

Charlotte used the extra key Nellie had given her to get into the house. She felt odd just walking in, knowing Andy was home. Nellie had insisted, though, saying he'd be upstairs in Ken's study, probably working on a proposal, and wouldn't want to be interrupted.

The house was quiet—the complete opposite of how it sounded when she'd left earlier that day. She checked the den and found Walker playing with a teething toy in his playpen. He gurgled sweetly, lifting his feet up as he tried to decide if he wanted his toes or the toy. She bent down to pick him up.

"Hey there, little fella. How was your afternoon?" He smiled at her tender tone. "You have a good nap while I was gone? I'm sure you did." She pulled the toy from his grip. "What's this? Can I have it?" she asked, pretending to put it in her mouth. Walker cooed, loving the interaction.

"Oh, you're back."

Charlotte startled and swirled around faster than she'd meant to, nearly losing her balance.

"Careful! Might not want to do that while you're holding my nephew." Andy stood there with his arms outstretched in anticipation of what could've happened.

"Hi," she said smiling, hoping to ease the sudden humiliation. The man was hard to figure out. He seemed so formal-like in conversation with his tone flat and boring, like he didn't care about anything. But yet, his eyes were wild, as if they were dancing behind that suit of his, waiting to hit on her. "Sorry. Guess you scared me."

"Just be careful next time. We don't want either one of you to get hurt now, do we?"

"Sure. Sorry." She placed Walker back in his playpen. "I hope I didn't disturb you. Nellie told me to come in without bothering you."

"It's fine," he said stiffly. "I was working, yes, but I needed a break. Heard you through the baby monitor." He pointed to the end table, where the green light on the monitor glowed.

"Oh. Um, thanks for watching him. I know how much Nellie appreciates it. I do, too. Gave me a chance to meet Mrs. Nelson." The wall clock chimed, signaling the top of the hour. "Now that I'm back, you're welcome to leave . . . or stay," she added quickly. "It's up to you."

He glanced at his watch and then down at the baby. "I think I'll hang out a little longer. It's not often I'm in town long enough to spend quality time with this little man."

"Sure, okay."

"Would you care to join us?" he asked, somewhat eagerly.

The thought of being alone with Andy Yates didn't sit too well with Charlotte. She liked Nicholas, quite a lot, and didn't want to jeopardize that relationship. She wasn't sure about this brother-in-law of Nellie's or his intentions.

God, how do I get out of this? I don't want to be alone with him, and I don't want to be rude.

"Um, thanks for the offer, but do you mind if I go for a walk instead? That is, if you're sure you want to stay?"

"That's fine. I'll be around for another hour or so. You better go ahead before it starts to rain, though. It's looking pretty dark out there." He peered through the blinds before walking around her to pick up his nephew, brushing his shoulder against hers as he did.

Charlotte moved toward the stairs slowly, watching the man and child. "Thanks. I'll just go change and then head out for a quick walk."

9:00 p.m.

It'd been a very long year. Vincent Cobb had chosen a path when the love of his life had lost her husband. It was a path he felt was necessary at the time. Had he known it would've ended the life of a teenage boy, he would've figured out something else to do. His end goal wouldn't have changed. He refused to be helpless, but he could've gotten to it differently. He couldn't change the past. He could only hope that God would forgive him. He knew Jesus, had known Him for years, but he allowed love for another to overpower him, to drive him to commit to something he now regretted. He'd pushed God to the side. The deeper he got into the double life he led, the further he got from the things of God. He became calloused to them.

He supplied prescription opioid painkillers from his veterinary clinic to a man who would, in turn, sell the drugs to users with chronic pain. He knew they were habit-forming. Yet he continued to supply.

Vincent had become hard or blind to what he was doing—that is, until he saw Charlotte. He was suddenly afraid, afraid for her life, of what Roland or Zeke might do to her, especially after she'd witnessed the accidental death. He could still see the kid—young, a future ahead of him, and then suddenly lifeless, lying in a pool of blood.

The night after it happened, Vincent came home and cried. His selfish thinking, of dealing with his helplessness the way he saw fit, had killed someone, someone innocent. He'd tossed and turned, flashes of the boy's vacant eyes and of the girl's horrified look shooting through his mind. She was innocent, too, and now she would die, just because she was in the wrong place at the wrong time.

He didn't sleep at all that night; and when he went hunting with Nicholas the next morning and saw the same girl in the woods, terror gripped him. Her appearance was that of a beating. His first thought was that Zeke had found her and tried killing her, but somehow, she'd escaped. That thought didn't change, even after they'd realized her memory was gone. A fist and a knife could've been the reasons behind those cuts and bruises.

It was that morning, the morning of the hunt, that he'd made up his mind to do what it took to protect the girl in the woods. He'd wanted to tell her who he was but he was afraid that she'd run again. If he knew where she was, he had a better chance of stepping in between her and his double life. But if she disappeared again, Vincent feared they'd find her before he did.

The silence ate at him, destroying a bit of him every day that he kept quiet. Once again, he'd made a selfish decision. Her protection wasn't the only reason he didn't speak. He was afraid for himself. He knew if she remembered, she'd recognize him; and she would talk.

He'd be caught and others, especially Nellie, would know what he'd been doing.

Sleepless nights and what-if days finally caught up with him. It was God's way of steadily nudging him in the right direction. Vincent decided he had to put his own selfishness aside. There was still a way to protect Charlotte if he was out of the picture. If the police chose to remove him, she could still possibly make it. Her memory. If she had it back, she would recognize him, yes, but she would also recognize Zeke, giving her an advantage to get away or share her information with a sketch artist.

The decision to tell Charlotte had been hard, but it was freeing. The fact that she forgave him and actually trusted him was indescribable. There were no words. He could not understand it at all.

God, I've messed up something awful, and I'm so sorry. I don't deserve Your forgiveness, and I don't deserve Charlotte's or anyone else's. Forgive me anyway . . . please. Help me to live *thank you, as Charlotte calls it, remembering daily why You died. Show me what to do.*

I'm just so selfish! Selfish! Selfish! Kept everything to myself just because I didn't want Nellie to know what I've become. I should've told the police about Charlotte when I found her in the woods—that she was in Jennings. Never should've tried to take matters into my own hands. Never should've agreed to go through with this whole thing without seeking Your will first.

That's it! No more of me doing it. You do it through me . . . if You'll use me.

CHAPTER SEVEN

Wednesday, April 13

6:15 a.m.

The ringing woke Nellie from a deep sleep.

"Hello," she said groggily.

"Hey, sis. I'm sorry if I woke you." Nicholas Nelson's voice was slow and steady. He was in big brother mode, protection status.

"When?" she asked, fully awake now.

"About twenty minutes ago," he said calmly. "I'm going to ask Sydney to watch the baby. She won't mind. You come on over when you're ready."

Nellie's shoulders began to shake. "No, Nick. I've got Andy. He'll want to be there for me, since Ken isn't. And you need Charlotte. I'll call Kelsey. She can take care of Walker."

Nicholas hesitated, feeling his chin quiver. "If you're sure and if Sydney wouldn't mind, that'd be nice."

"See you in about an hour." Nellie hung up the phone and looked to the ceiling.

He's gone, God.

She sat up, drawing her knees to her chest and sobbed.

9:20 a.m.

Nicholas and Charlotte sat under the gazebo in the hospital court-yard. The Wednesday morning was already warm, and the scent of freshly cut grass filled the air. She silently prayed for the Nelson family, especially the man beside her. They were all struggling, as she still was over the death of her own father. But the Nelson children's struggles ran deep, different from their mother's.

Mrs. Nelson grieved the loss of a husband. He would no longer be around to comfort her after a hard day or laugh with her into the night. He wouldn't walk into the kitchen early in the mornings, hair tussled and slippers scraping across the wood flooring. His time of a whispered *I love you* or a stolen kiss had passed. They'd never celebrate another anniversary or birthday together. His side of the bed would remain cold from now on. Nick Nelson was gone from this Earth. All that remained was the memory of him, of pictures and stories that would be told for years to come.

Nellie's and Nicholas' grieving was much worse. They grieved for the memory of their father and the loss of his body. But they mourned with deep sorrow over the loss of his soul.

Nicholas had been with him when he took his last breath. He'd cried out to God for his father to hear the words and to accept them. He did nothing silently during those last minutes with him. If he had something to say to the nurse, he spoke loudly. If he had something to say to himself or to God, he made sure it could be heard from the next room. And when he explained God's unconditional love, the sacrifice of His Son for mankind, the fact that death could not keep Jesus in the grave and the forgiveness He offered, Nicholas wept bitterly. He begged and pleaded with his unresponsive father as loud as he could.

He didn't want to take a chance that the reason Nick wasn't responding was a lack of hearing. If he did not accept Jesus now, he'd spend eternity separated from God.

He cried out to God. He yelled at his father. He chided himself for not saying more when he'd had the chance. He apologized to anyone listening for taking the coward's way out.

Nicholas knew his words on salvation had upset his father in the past. He'd felt the rejection of a father's love and backed off. Now, looking down at the eternally lost man before him, he realized his dad wasn't rejecting him but rejecting the one, true God. He never should've allowed his personal feelings of keeping the peace between them to interfere. What good had that done either of them now?

He'd looked up, not able to see through the water in his eyes. "I'm so, so sorry, God. I was so busy trying to run from confrontation that I failed You. You were ridiculed. You were beaten. You were humiliated by Your own inner circle. You dealt with all of that before even going to the cross. I faced only a few hurtful words that weren't even directed at me, but at You. Forgive me for my lack of strength, for my misunderstanding. Open Dad's heart and his mind to You. Don't let him go, please! Not until he's saved! Please, oh please, Lord."

Nicholas had never shown this side of himself to his dad. Even he had never seen this side of himself. It was the only time he'd poured all he had into another individual. He wasn't fighting for someone's life. He was fighting for someone's soul. He'd held his father's hand and stroked it, reverting to childlike desperation.

"Please, Dad. Please. Believe Jesus. Please, Daddy. It's your last chance. If you don't . . . oh, please, please."

The son of the tough, stubborn man beseeched his Heavenly Father and his earthly father for endless moments. The story in Second Samuel of King David pleading for days for his son's life, the son born out of adultery, filled Nicholas' mind. They were calling out to the same God. He was just as real to a king as He was to Nicholas. He knew the decision was God's—whether his dad lived or died—and he knew he did not doubt God's power to change Nick Nelson's eternal outcome, even at the last minute in a comatose state. He also knew that like King David, he would worship the Lord in the midst of sorrow, no matter the ending.

With an outstretched heart, he'd bowed his head. The alarms on the machines sounded, screaming into the room. Nicholas had lifted his eyes as Nick Nelson's lines flattened.

Doctors and nurses rushed in, pushing Nicholas aside. They checked monitors. They checked IVs and breathing tubes. They checked the patient for a pulse. Nothing. There was no living response. It was out of their hands. There was nothing they could do. The time of death was called.

Nicholas had stood there, staring at the now-lifeless form of his once strong-willed and so very hardheaded father. He'd slowly slid down the wall, bringing his knees to his chest and his hands to his face as he hit the floor. He'd wept uncontrollably as the hospital staff quietly bustled around his father, removing wires and tubes.

Oh, Lord. He's gone. There's no hope for him now.

A nurse, unaware of the inner struggle in Nicholas' mind and of the spiritual warfare that had taken place within the four walls just minutes before, gently swiped the cheek of the lifeless patient with her thumb, where a single tear had fallen and dried.

CHAPTER EIGHT

Thursday, April 21

After Nick Nelson's funeral, life seemed a mess, but the Nelsons made an attempt at normal. Patricia Nelson put on her famously strong façade. She eased back into her life of friends and community functions, still representing her family with grace and style. For the time being, she'd decided to stay with Nellie, hoping the two of them could lean on each other for a while. Nellie returned to work and with the help of her mother, fed the few friends and family who happened to show up for dinner. Nicholas went back to teaching and busied himself the best he could with lesson plans and thoughts of Charlotte.

Detective Jones checked in with Charlotte often, making sure she was still okay staying in Jennings for, hopefully, just a few more days. He said the man they were trying to nail was in town. That realization added to her growing fear as each day passed with no arrests made. But she assured him she'd stay. She'd been released from Dr. Mitchell's care and could physically and medically go home; but if she didn't see this thing through to the end, she worried she'd spend the rest of her life looking over her shoulder. To top it off, there was no one to go home to, no one she was longing to see.

With her mind made up, Charlotte started working for the Cranes at their small shop in the middle of town. It sold mainly cards for all occasions and small novelty gifts. It felt nice to work, even if it was short-lived.

To give Nellie and her mother some alone time and to ease her mind of putting them in danger, Charlotte moved into the only extended-stay lodging Jennings had to offer. The small location was simple but comfortable and not too expensive. Plus, Charlotte didn't feel like she was in anyone's way there. She could come and go as she pleased, not worried about overstepping her boundaries with gracious hosts or intruding on much-needed family time.

Andy was to leave on another business trip in about a week, but had told Nellie he'd be willing to postpone it if she needed him. He prided himself on taking on part of the role his younger brother held. Nellie was family, with or without Ken. She hadn't given him her answer yet.

Vincent seemed much more relaxed around Charlotte. He came by and visited frequently, checking on her and making sure there wasn't anything she needed. During one of his visits, Charlotte found out that Vincent and Detective Jones had been in constant communication for a year. Supposedly, he was some sort of informant, but the detective couldn't let her know that in the beginning. He was afraid it would blow Vincent's cover.

All the parties had been identified, even Roland. But they still didn't have any hard evidence to convict him, other than Vincent's testimony. He was sneaky and intelligent. His instructions came through the mail, typed and without a return address. The postmark was never from the same place twice. Vincent had never been able to catch Roland's voice on tape when he was discussing something illegal. Other than through the mail, when Roland did have something to say about a job, he called Zeke, and Zeke called Vincent. He kept Vincent at arm's length for a reason. He talked to him, but his conversations with the man were everyday ones, not of breaking the law.

Though he'd shared a lot of information and was kind and they'd actually become pretty good friends, Charlotte felt Vincent was still a bit reserved. There was something he wasn't telling her, and she couldn't shake the feeling of what came with that possible omission.

But what she did know connected her to him, whether she was comfortable with the feeling or not. After all, they shared a secret that, for the time being, needed to be kept; and other than Detective Jones, he was her only outlet to talk it through.

Vincent had warned her over and over how dangerous things could get, hoping to convince her to forget about staying and to take the police up on their witness protection offer. She considered it but always came to the same conclusion. She'd rather be living her life with some distant protection—for they continued to keep tabs on her—than living a fake life with enhanced protection. Her life, her own stories and memories, were too precious to her now that she had them back to go without them again.

The warnings Vincent issued, however, sent unbelievable moments of terror through her mind daily. She tried to control the possible what-ifs when they came, but she found the job uncontrollable. She had to let the moments run their course, as hard as they were. They passed eventually, but always returned sooner than she liked.

Overall, Charlotte found she enjoyed small-town life. She met new people each day, enjoying the different personalities. The traffic wasn't bad. The church was welcoming. There was even a quiet route, where she could run through a wooded neighborhood behind the extended-stay. Besides her fear, she was content. During the days, she hung out with Nicholas, worked at the shop from ten to four, went for a run, relaxed at the extended-stay, or spent time with Nellie and Walker.

In the evenings, she thought of her father and of Mr. Nelson. She missed her father greatly and cried herself to sleep several nights, but she knew she'd see him again. She knew their separation wasn't final. Nicholas didn't have that luxury. He didn't know if what he'd said in those last moments had made a difference. He only knew what had transpired between them in the past before the heart attack. He kept his feelings and concerns on the subject to himself, but Charlotte knew they ate at him, as they would her if the roles were reversed.

3:57 p.m.

"Hey you," called Nicholas as he walked through the glass doors of Mr. and Mrs. Crane's shop.

Charlotte looked up from the box of Mother's Day cards she was unloading. "Hey yourself," she said and smiled. "How was your day? The kids behave, or did you have to turn into one of those superhero figurines on your desk to control them?"

He chuckled. "Funny you should ask. Today was a Hulk day, unfortunately. Started out calm, but by the end, they broke loose, so I had to break loose."

"Sorry to hear that. I would not want to see the Hulk side of Nicholas Nelson," she teased, though she knew it meant he'd had a rough day. "So, what brings you by?"

"Well," he said checking his watch, "it's three till four, about quittin' time. I was hoping I could convince you to join me for a little outing. I'll have you back by ten-thirty, I promise."

"That doesn't sound very little."

"It's little in the fact that it won't cost much, and it's around town," he replied with a wink.

"Oh, okay, sure. Just give me a minute. Gladys is in the back. Let me tell her I'm leaving. How do I look? Do I need to walk over to my place and change?" she asked, waving her hand in front of herself, as a model does to show off a particular item for sell.

He studied her for a second. "Nope, you look good to me."

"Very funny," she said. Her khaki pants, mint green short-sleeve blouse, and brown flats would have to do. Nicholas obviously didn't want to waste time with an outfit change. "I'll be right back."

Charlotte disappeared into the back to tell the owner she was leaving. He watched her go. She was beautiful, and she got prettier every time he saw her. He hadn't normally been a fan of a woman in glasses; but on Charlotte, he wouldn't have it any other way. The rims were rectangular-shaped, making her look intelligent, sweet, and stunning.

"All right," she called, appearing from the back room. "I'm good to go."

"Great. It'll be fun; just wait and see." He reached for her hand and interlocked their fingers.

"I have no doubt," she beamed.

They pulled onto a dirt road, eventually leading to a dusty brown house and barn on several acres of land. A scent of manure and musty hay entered Charlotte's nose.

"Where are we?" she asked. A cluster of beautiful horses gathered near a barbed fence. In the distance, two more grazed in the field behind.

"This is the place of one of Dad's old college buddies, Mr. Fred Manor. He's a kind man, who never had any family. My sister and I used to come out here all the time as kids, riding horses or helping him pick up pinecones from his yard. Then we'd sit on the porch, drinking sweet tea as we listened to the baseball game on the radio. I guess you could say he kind of adopted the two of us."

"He sounds like a fun uncle type, happy to spoil his family," she smiled.

He looked off into the distance, remembering those times when his father would join them on those horse rides. It was one time when he felt like he was on equal ground with his dad. They didn't butt heads, question one another, or try to convince the other he was wrong about an issue. They just rode, feeling the breeze and smelling the pine trees.

Nicholas nodded. "Yep, that's exactly what he was like. Still is, if we let him. In fact, I called him during my break this morning and asked if he'd mind having a couple horses saddled and ready to go by four-fifteen."

"You've got to be kidding me, Nicholas! I can't ride." Charlotte pointed to herself. "Look at me. I'm not dressed for horses!"

He laughed. "Like I said, you look good to me. You asked how you looked, not if what you were wearing was appropriate for what we were doing."

"You just think you're so funny, don't you," she snapped in jest. "Well, I'll tell you what then. Since I bought only a few things because I plan to head home soon, you can just buy me a replacement outfit if this one gets ruined." She stared at him, as he said nothing. "It will be your fault if it gets messed up. You should've warned me."

Nicholas wrapped his arm around her shoulders and pulled her in for a hug. He kissed the top of her head, whispering, "I'll buy you another one if needed. It's worth the risk to see your reaction."

Charlotte jokingly pushed him away. "I may mess it up on purpose, you know."

"And I may purposely let you. It would mean a shopping date with the prettiest girl in Georgia."

"Oh, you're hopeless!"

He laughed as they walked, heading toward the horses. They were magnificent creatures up close. Charlotte hadn't realized how big they were until she was standing a few feet from one. She noticed a bluish-gray one and a brown one were saddled.

She pointed. "Are we riding these two?"

"Yep. That one," he nodded, "will be yours. She's an older mare. Pretty gentle these days. I'll ride the bay. He's a little younger, and probably still just as safe. But I'd prefer to be on him in case he gets spooked."

Charlotte walked over to her horse. "That's fine with me. Mine's a beauty." She reached up and stroked her mane. "What's her name?"

"Uh, that one is Bruise."

She crinkled her nose, causing her glasses to slide just a bit. "That's a horrible name for such a lovely horse."

"All right, if she were yours, what would you name her?" he asked, curiously.

"Well, let's see." She backed up to get a better look of the whole horse. She was strong. Her muscles were defined. The animal lifted her head as if to say she was also confident. Charlotte could understand why the name Bruise was chosen. The color of the horse definitely looked like a bruise when it was first forming. She smiled. She could use the color *and* the strength.

"Storm. I'd call her Storm."

Nicholas stooped, holding his hands together, forming a cup. "Storm does sound like a better name for her. Maybe I will suggest it to Mr. Manor. Now, put your foot in my hands, and I'll give you a boost. As you're going up, swing your other leg over the saddle."

She looked at him cautiously. "Can I not just step into the stirrups?"

He stood. "Yeah, you can. I just thought it would be more fun—"

Charlotte was on Bruise before he finished the sentence. He laughed out loud. "Guess I shouldn't assume anything with you. Never underestimate the strength of a runner."

Nicholas talked Charlotte through the ride, the mechanics and tempo. He showed her how to hold the reins and what commands to say when. She was a quick study, seemingly enjoying the new adventure. Most beginners didn't pick up on horseback riding so easily.

He watched her turn the horse at the end of the property and shift her weight accordingly when the soreness in her backside became too much. He saw her growing in confidence as she learned to take Bruise from a walk to a trot. She was having a great time. He was, too.

He'd grown very fond of this woman, so much so that she tended to make everything better, just by being there. Over the last two weeks, they'd laughed, and they'd cried. They'd learned each other's deepest regrets. They'd seen each other's reactions as they handled some of the most difficult scenarios life had to offer. They'd already experienced the range of emotions a couple might go through after being together for twenty years. They'd lived with the fear she'd felt in the woods to the loss of her memory to the rejoicing of its return, to the deaths of each of their fathers, to the struggle of his still unsaved mother. Through it all, they seemed to grow closer together. He hadn't expressed his future intentions toward her yet, but somehow, he felt she already knew them.

Charlotte Hallaway was the kind of woman he could spend the rest of his life with. She was kind, smart, strong, and funny. She loved the Lord, and she adored his family, especially Nellie and Walker.

Thank You, God, for bringing Sydney into my life when You did. Your timing is always perfect.

"Whoa, Bruise. Whoa." Charlotte pulled her horse next to his. "She's fantastic. This has been a first for me, but wow! I think I've just found something I like that comes awfully close to hot dogs."

Nicholas hollered with laughter. "You're not right, you know that?" Charlotte leaned forward, patting Bruise's neck and smiled wide enough to see her white, slightly crooked teeth. With Nicholas, she was happy, genuinely happy.

"So what were you in such deep thought about a second ago?" she asked.

"You."

"Me?" she questioned, eyeing him curiously.

"Yep, you. Just thinking about how amazing you are. Actually, I was thanking God for you, for bringing you here when He did." Nicholas descended first, and then helped Charlotte down.

"And what a grand entry . . . bus accident, memory loss, horrible headache, messed up ankle, and a night in strange woods."

"It'll make for a great story on how we met." He grinned.

Nicholas knew Charlotte wasn't questioning God's will. He knew she was grateful to be in Jennings and was happy she'd met him and

Nellie. But he also knew there was an underlying issue she'd yet to reveal about herself. There wasn't a reason for her to still be in Jennings. She kept saying she just didn't want to go home yet, but there had to be more to it.

He knew she had sporadic nightmares and periodic bouts of sudden fear. She'd told him about the nightmares when he'd question her tiredness one day. But what she'd said was vague. Just that the dreams upset her. Though she tried to keep them from him, Nicholas could tell they were intense, disturbing images. He'd seen the sudden fears often as her eyes darkened and her body shook. It happened for no apparent reason and at any moment. One minute, they were out for a walk, laughing and cutting up. The next minute, Charlotte was quiet, almost afraid to speak, and shivering as if a burst of cold air had just crossed her skin. He wondered if she'd seen something or suddenly remembered something that brought her to a dark point in her past. He wanted to ask her about it when she showed the fear, but he couldn't. Something told him to wait it out, that she'd talk to him when she was ready.

"So," she said brushing the horse's hair off her shins, "what's next? It's only five-thirty, and you said we'd be out until after ten."

Nicholas took the reins from both animals and made his way to the stable. He called out over his shoulder as Charlotte continued to inspect her outfit. "Well, I guess we're headed to the mall first." He laughed. "And then I was thinking a picnic and outdoor movie."

Charlotte lifted her attention to her date. "Really? Where? How?"

"I've got a friend setting it up in the center of the high school's soccer field."

"That's so neat, Nicholas." She ran to catch up with him. "Thank you. Thanks for these wonderful first-time adventures. I wouldn't want to spend them with anyone else." She glowed with sheer enjoyment.

"Me neither." He gathered the reins into one hand and turned to face her. She was windblown and dirty, yet she was the most amazingly beautiful person he'd ever seen, inside and out. Nicholas tucked a piece of hair behind her ear and leaned in for a soft kiss.

CHAPTER NINE

Friday, April 22

1:30 p.m.

"Okay, Charlotte, I think I'm ready. You sure you have everything under control before I run some errands?" asked Gladys Crane as she stepped into view from the back room.

Charlotte straightened the stack of today's mail, pushing it to the side as she did. She looked around the store, making sure she didn't have any unanswered questions. "Yes, ma'am, I think I'm good." The empty table in the corner caught her eye. "Oh, what about that?" she pointed. "What would you like me to put on it?"

Gladys glanced over at the table. "Oh, yes. I'm sorry. I forgot to mention we should have a delivery sometime this afternoon. I'm expecting some additional Mother's Day gifts. If it comes while you're here, just sign for it and leave the box under the front counter. I'll take care of the unpacking when I return."

"I don't mind unpacking it for you, Mrs. Gladys."

"If you're sure you don't mind, I'd really appreciate it. Those jobs tend to keep me late, and I was actually hoping to leave right at closing time tonight. Bob wants to take me out to dinner," she replied, and then blushed. "It's our fortieth anniversary."

Charlotte grinned with delight for the dear woman. "That's wonderful. Why don't I just stay and lock up for you? That way, you'll have

186

a chance to do something afterwards, too, if you want. Catch a movie or something. And don't worry about paying me for the extra time. Just call it an anniversary gift."

Gladys put her hands over her mouth. "My dear, are you sure?"

"Absolutely. It's not a problem. You and Mr. Bob enjoy yourselves," she encouraged.

"Well, if you're sure." Gladys handed Charlotte the store key. "I'll take you up on it before you change your mind." She clapped her hands in excitement. "Oh, Bob will be thrilled. Thank you, Charlotte."

Charlotte nodded sweetly. "Happy Anniversary," she called as her employer made her way out of the store. Charlotte laughed to herself. She silently prayed she'd be that happy and that grateful to be with her husband after forty years. The Cranes were an inspirational couple.

Charlotte piddled around the little shop, doing what she could between the small number of customers trickling in and out. She swept the floors and dusted any open areas not already filled with merchandise. She organized the new catalogues that'd come in during the week. She checked the greeting cards and returned out-of-place ones to their rightful spot. Children tended to pick up a card, scan the inside, and put it back wherever they were standing. It was usually close, but not quite in the correct place.

Charlotte was looking for a particular sympathy card's home when a delivery truck pulled up in front of the shop. She found the card's spot just as Nicholas appeared, holding the door for the delivery man. The man had a hard time seeing around the large box.

"Hold up," Nicholas said as he grabbed a corner of the box long enough to steady it. "Okay, a little to your left, and you should be in the clear," he directed.

He glanced over his shoulder and winked at Charlotte, who was watching him in surprise. She could see the shopping bag from a women's clothing store in his free hand. Last night, they hadn't been able to find her size. She wondered if he'd gone and bought something anyway. She smiled to herself. Nicholas Nelson was a thoughtful man, to be sure.

"Thanks, dude. She 'bout got away from me there. Sure woulda been a mess if she had—broken glass and an earful back at the office."

Charlotte froze. She couldn't move. She knew that voice.

"You got it?" Nicholas asked, still holding the door.

"Yep. Think I'm through." He shifted his hands on the box. "This is kinda heavy. Where you want it?"

Nicholas turned to Charlotte for some instruction. His shoulders dropped. The look he'd seen so many times before had once again found her. But this time it was different. She wasn't just afraid. She was truly terrified, immobile from the fear.

He sighed, worried about her. "Uh, I guess over there," he answered, gesturing. "To your right is good."

"Okay." The man dropped the box to the ground. Something rattled. Nicholas silently grunted, hoping nothing had broken. The man picked up the clipboard on top of the box and waved it in the air. "So, who's signing?" he asked, getting his first look at the room.

He saw her and pointed the clipboard in her direction. "You?"

Charlotte stared at him, unable to find her words. It was him. It was Vincent's partner. He was in her place of business, asking her a question. Could he hurt her here? With the police hiding in the shadows?

She needed to speak, but it was like her tongue was made of lead. Her mouth became temporarily paralyzed.

She needed him to leave, to get away from her. Maybe he didn't recognize her. Maybe he hadn't gotten as good a look at her as Vincent had. She blinked several times, trying to shake herself out of her immobile state. "Um," she forced out quietly, "yes, I'll sign."

He slowly walked over to her and handed her the board and attached pen. She accepted it cautiously, signing *Veruca Woods*, and handed it back to him.

"Thanks," he said looking at her intently with beady eyes. He nodded to Nicholas and returned to his truck. Not until the man drove away did Charlotte take her first real breath.

Nicholas walked over to her. "Hey, you," he said, wrapping her in a shielding hug. "You okay?" He'd never asked her the reasoning behind her episodes before; but this time, it was different. This time, it was deeper, much deeper.

Beads of sweat formed on her forehead, but she shook her head, trying hard to push the incident to the side. She didn't want Nicholas to know, not yet. Detective Jones had cautioned her not to tell anyone. But she'd have to tell him soon. Everyone would know before the week's end, she predicted. The conclusion to why she'd ended up in Jennings, Georgia, was coming, and quickly. Her life, once again, was in danger.

The words stammered out of her mouth. "I-I-I'm fine. Just a lot on my mind." She pulled away from his embrace. "It's," she struggled to change the subject, "it's not quitting time. Why are you here?"

He lifted the bag onto the counter. She'd already forgotten about it. "Well, we had early dismissal today, so I felt like a little shopping."

"In a women's store?" she asked, raising heavy eyebrows.

"Yeah, sure. Why not?" He handed her the bag. Inside, she found two pairs of pants—khakis to match the ones she wore on her horseback riding date and a pair of dressy gray slacks. Her hands continued to shake as she checked the labels. They were the right size and would be easy to wash. Charlotte looked up at him in surprise.

Nicholas threw his hands in the air. "Okay, okay, so I cheated a little. I took Nellie out to a late lunch in exchange for shopping help."

"That makes more sense." She smiled weakly.

The vision of the deliveryman wouldn't go away. Her mind kept replaying the scene of him knocking that poor kid to his death. All she saw was red blood pouring out of his head. Shivers shot down her spine as she reached for the stool next to the wall. "Thank you," she replied faintly. "They're great." Charlotte sat on the stool, feeling the color fade from her face.

Nicholas grabbed her shoulders, getting a closer look at her eyes. "Hey there, you don't look so good." He glanced at the clock above their heads. It said three-fifteen, forty-five minutes before the usual shift change. "Why don't I call Gladys and see if she can come on back to the store now. Then I'll take you to your place so you can get some rest."

She tried to straighten, shaking her head. "No, don't do that. It's their anniversary, and I told her I'd close up tonight. I'll be fine. There's no need to ruin their anniversary over a little weakness on my part." She looked down at the ground, gripping the sides of the stool. "Just give me a minute. I'll be okay." Charlotte heard his grunt of disapproval.

"If that's what you want to do, fine. But I'm not going anywhere. I'll wait here with you until you're ready to go." He scanned his surroundings. "Are there any sodas in here?"

She nodded faintly. "There's a refrigerator in the back. Should be something in there."

"Good." He lifted her arms, causing her to stand, and then gently guided her to the ground, resting her back against the wall. "I'd feel more comfortable if you were down here while I step away. Don't want my girl falling if she passes out."

He winked, trying to lighten the mood.

"Your girl, huh?" she asked weakly. Her eyes slowly closed.

"Yes, ma'am. You don't object, do you?"

"Too tired to object right now."

He smiled. "I'll take it." Nicholas disappeared into the back room in search of a soda.

Zeke drove away from the Crane's place, an excited smile stretching across his face. He'd found her. The girl from the superstore was here, in Jennings. How had he not run into her before? He didn't live in Jennings, but he lived in a bordering county and had routes all over this place. What luck! If that other guy hadn'ta been there, he could've said something. He could've threatened her.

Vinnie kept telling him she hadn't gotten a good look at them, that she wouldn't be able to identify them. But from what Zeke just saw, that was clearly not the case. She recognized him! He needed to tell Roland—now. He'd know what to do 'cause they'd be in it for sure if she went to the police.

It made no sense, though. If she'd seen them, why hadn't she already gone to the cops? Was she no good with descriptions? Or maybe she was too scared, 'cause she knew they'd seen her, too. Zeke held on to that last thought. He needed her to be so afraid that she stayed far away from the cops.

He shook his head. But now, she knew where to find him. She didn't know his name, but she could make the connection to where he worked and then ask around. She could have him nailed by the end of the day, if she knew how. They'd have to work quickly or leave town and disappear. If they disappeared, they'd be free of the law, but not of Roland. He'd hunt them down and make them pay for screwing up his business. Zeke thought about it. Better to end up in prison than dead on the streets somewhere.

Maybe, just maybe, he'd get lucky and get to her before she worked up enough nerve to go for help. Alive and free was an even better option. He picked up the clipboard he'd thrown on the passenger side seat. What was her name? Veruca Woods. That's a name you don't hear every day. People would definitely know the name. It stood out like a sore thumb. It was a start.

6:00 p.m.

At six o'clock exactly, Nicholas Nelson escorted Charlotte out of the Crane's store. Her color had returned with the soda. She'd finished her job without too much trouble, unpacking the box that'd been delivered. She joked with him and smiled politely, but Nicholas knew she was still struggling. He could see it in her eyes, no matter how hard she disguised her feelings with normal behavior.

"Nicholas?" she asked, locking the store.

"Yeah?"

"You mind taking me to get a bite to eat? I'm not real hungry, but I don't think I'm quite ready to go back to my room yet."

"Do I mind?" he jested. "Do I mind spending more time than I thought I'd get to with a freckled-faced beauty who loves fall and daisies? Who loves strangely named horses and runs for the fun of it? Let me see." He tapped his finger on his chin. "If I must, I must. But, man! What a way to spoil an evening. I guess mopping the kitchen floor will just have to wait until next weekend."

"Very funny. If you'd rather spend time with your linoleum, just say so. Don't do me any favors," she teased.

"I'll have you know, my kitchen floor is of the highest quality linoleum, and I work hard to keep that fresh-from-the-store shine." He wrapped his arm around her shoulder as they walked to his truck. "But absence makes the heart grow fonder, right?" He leaned down, kissing the top of her head.

She laughed. "I'll take your word for it."

"So, what do you feel like? Cafeteria food—minus the antiseptic—drive-thru hamburger, or sit-down steak?"

"Can we do a drive-thru somewhere and then park to eat?"

"If we must," he poked.

"Dude, she's here!"

"Who's here?" asked Vincent, holding the phone loosely to his ear.

"The girl. The witness." Zeke talked faster than usual.

Vincent ran his hand through his shaggy blond hair, gritting his teeth. Zeke had found her? How? He'd been so careful not to say anything when they'd spoken over the last two weeks. Part of him had hoped she'd been all but forgotten. It'd been over fourteen days, and nothing had happened. Zeke had even quit obsessing over finding her. What had changed?

"Seriously?" asked Vincent. "How? Where?"

"Pure luck! Made a delivery to a store in Jennings an' she was there, workin' it. And I'm tellin' ya, man," he stressed, "she recognized me. I know it."

Vincent dropped on his couch, disbelief washing over him. "How do you know? There's no way."

"She did. Just had that look, ya know? Like she seen a ghost."

"Oh." He couldn't believe this was happening. "What are you going to do?"

"Since she recognized me, she can figure me out through work. We gotta get to her before she does. I called Roland as soon as I left the store. He said he'd take care of it." Zeke paused. "Don't think he trusts us no more when it comes to this girl."

Sweat dripped off Vincent's forehead. "Zeke, what *exactly* did you tell Roland?"

"I told 'im what she looks like. Not too tall, wears glasses, and has brown hair. And man, does she have a bunch of freckles 'cross that nose. Looks like a connect-the-dot picture. Oh, and her name. I told him her name." He laughed. "Can you believe it? The first time I seen her, and she's gotta sign off on a delivery. It was genius! I couldn't a thought of a better plan myself."

Zeke gloated over his find as Vincent felt sick to his stomach. "So . . . what *is* her name?"

He hollered. "Get this. It's Veruca Woods. Crazy, huh? What a name. I'm tellin' ya, we couldn't a had better luck. I mean, ya hear that name, and ya won't forget it. Shouldn't take long to ask around and find out where she's stayin' at."

Vincent breathed his first sigh of relief. Charlotte hadn't written her real name. She hadn't even written the name they'd given her when her memory was gone. She'd chosen one of the ones she'd rejected. And she added *Woods* because that's where she'd been found. In her fear, she'd had a clear thought. She was sending Vincent a message. That message was that she had been found out. Charlotte figured Zeke would contact Vincent immediately after seeing her. It covered her back—both their backs—in case she couldn't get to him first to warn him.

A horrible thought crossed his mind. What if Zeke was tailing her now? Was he waiting outside the grocery store or gas station where she'd popped in to purchase a drink or something? Even worse, what if he was waiting outside her place at the extended-stay right now, sitting in his vehicle while talking to him? What if he was waiting for Roland, so he could tell her which door he'd seen her go in?

"Zeke," he said as calmly as he could, "where are you? Do you have eyes on Veruca now?"

"No," Zeke replied with a pout. "Had to finish m' route. Roland said he'd take care of the situation. I told 'im I'd dump the delivery truck on the side of the road and watch her from 'cross the street 'til she left. But he said if I don't show up for my stops, it'd put my name on alert if somethin' went accidentally wrong, if you know what I mean."

Vincent knew exactly what he meant. Charlotte was in danger. Roland planned to get rid of her. "So, where's Roland right now?"

"Aw, he's out with his family for supper. He's playin' the whole 'I've got this covered' attitude pretty cool. Agrees she can't really hide in too many places with a name like Veruca." Zeke actually sounded disappointed that he wasn't invited to help in the disposal of the witness. "Acted like he'd have her found in a day or two."

Vincent's heart raced. *It may be sooner than that.* "Zeke, I've got to go. Let me know if you hear anything else from Roland."

"Sure, man. See ya."

6:20 p.m.

Charlotte tried keeping her cool, but she doubted she was doing a very good job of it. She'd asked Nicholas to take her through a drive-thru and to eat in the truck so she could get a sense of whether or not she was being followed. She pulled down the visor mirror, pretending to check her makeup. Between it and the passenger side mirror, she had a pretty solid view. Occasionally, she'd glance to her left and over her shoulder to make sure she hadn't missed anything.

Either Zeke was an excellent tail, or she hadn't been followed. It was still plenty light enough to see the color of cars and the drivers themselves. Vehicles turned off or joined the light traffic. They passed Nicholas, pulling in front of him or beside him, and he passed them, doing the same. No one stayed very long in one position. Traffic moved normally. She saw nothing suspicious or out of the ordinary.

Detective Jones said they'd be following her, watching over her. She knew it, but still felt uneasy. She hadn't noticed Zeke following them, but she hadn't spotted the police either. Once she'd gained control, she'd called the detective from the back of the store to update him, not long after Zeke had left. She told him she recognized Vincent's partner, but she wasn't sure he'd recognized her. He seemed awfully collected if he had. The detective again gave her the option to get out, especially now that she'd seen him, but she chose to continue. Vincent was on her side now. She wanted this whole thing to be over, and she wondered if she got out how long that would take. She knew the man's face now, knew where he worked. He was no longer in the wind.

Although Charlotte had told the police she remembered what Zeke looked like, Vincent wanted to be certain—for her safety. He'd wanted to draw Zeke out in the open, to give Charlotte a chance to look at him from a distance to make sure her memory of him was correct. She needed to recognize the man before he recognized her. But Zeke followed orders, which made it impossible to draw him out. He met up with Vincent only when Roland instructed, usually the day of a drug exchange. The plans were given by Roland and executed by Zeke and Vincent. Neither discussed anything over the phone but their job. They weren't to see each other and until today, Vincent had no idea where Zeke spent his time. The police had never informed him of that information, even though they were fully aware.

They pulled up to the menu. "So, what looks good?" asked Nicholas. She studied the choices. There were pictures of hamburgers, chicken strips, and grilled cheese sandwiches. She glanced over at the desserts, assorted milkshakes, and chocolate chip cookies. "Um, I'm really not too hungry, but I am a bit hot." The constant paranoia had caused her body temperature to rise. "How about a peach milkshake?"

He smiled. "Sounds like the perfect supper. I think I'll join you, but I'll have a strawberry one with an order of fries."

Nicholas pulled up to the speaker. He placed his order and drove around to the window. The lane from the speaker to the window narrowed. She felt trapped between the restaurant on their left; the tall, overlapping bushes on their right; and cars in front and behind them.

The tight space made Charlotte nervous. She struggled to catch her breath. If Zeke was following her, there'd be nowhere for her to run.

Part of Psalm twenty-three popped into her head. *Even though I walk through the valley of the shadow of death, I will fear no evil, for you are with me.* She repeated it to herself over and over, substituting *walk through* with *drive through*, until Nicholas' truck was parked in an open space.

Nicholas pulled the straws from the bag, handing Charlotte hers and sinking his into his pink shake. He stirred the strawberry chunks as he swirled his straw in a circle. The cup was cold, so he wrapped a napkin around it as a buffer. Charlotte was coming off another bout of fear. He'd seen it kick in after he ordered. Her grip around the purse in her lap had tightened. He waited to speak until he noticed her grip loosening a minute or two after they'd gotten their food.

"You still hot? If you want, press this." He pointed to a button in front of her. "It can heat your seat *or* cool it."

She leaned forward and pressed it. Cool air immediately released.

"A truck of all trades, huh?"

"I guess so," he said softly. "Nan told me to keep it. She didn't want to have to look at it sitting in the driveway every day—on the days she actually makes it to her own house."

"You okay with that? You're seeing it every day?" Charlotte asked, compassion slowly filling her voice over fear.

He thought about it for a minute. "You know, I am. I let it serve as a reminder we should never take God for granted. He could call us home at any time, and we need to be ready."

"Very true," she exhaled.

God, control this. I want to cry because I'm so scared, but I need to keep that hidden. Nicholas isn't supposed to know yet.

"Your mom's been on my mind lately, for that reason," Charlotte whispered as she placed her purse in the backseat, getting it out of the way in case she spilled milkshake on it and giving herself a second to calm down. "Every time I think of my dad, I remember your dad, and it breaks my heart. I pray he heard you before he died." Nicholas sighed. He prayed the same prayer daily. "I hurt for your mom. She doesn't know God. She's dealing with your dad's death without Him."

Nicholas hesitated with his food, close to losing his appetite. "I know. But the fact that she's not quite as stubborn as he was gives me hope. I've mentioned my beliefs to her casually since Dad's funeral. I wanted to test her out. I wanted to see if she'd cut me off and refuse to speak to me. That's basically what Dad did, you know?" Charlotte nodded. "He talked about what *he* wanted to discuss, but *my* topics were pretty much off-limits."

"And how did she react?"

He smiled faintly. "Well, Nan asked a few questions. She took it in like she would at one of her functions with a guest speaker on the latest charities. She'll probably do some research on what I said." He paused. "Honestly, I think she'll come to the Truth. She'll just be very careful and hesitant about it, since Dad was so against God."

That bit of encouragement was good to hear. Charlotte contemplated what Nicholas went through with his mother. She didn't have family anymore. They'd all died. But thankfully, she hadn't worried about their salvation and where they'd spend eternity. Her mom, dad, and brother had all known Christ. She'd see them all again in Heaven. That knowledge made her sleep easier at night. But Nicholas didn't have that comfort.

She cleared her throat. "I hope you chose not to order a full meal because you wanted to, not because I didn't. It won't bother me to watch you eat," Charlotte said as she quickly peeled the tip of her straw paper. "I mean, I could've cracked a window to get rid of the smell." Before he could answer, she blew through the opened portion, sending the paper flying at Nicholas' cheek.

"Hey," he said, bringing his hand up to cover an invisible wound. "What's the big idea? Distract a fella with guilt talk and then ambush him?"

She laughed. "Sorry, old habit of my father's. I needed something to smile about."

"Yeah, well, now you've done it. You have just unleashed the beast. When you least expect it, something will come your way." He grinned, enjoying seeing her loosen up a little.

But she didn't. Her face darkened again, and her knuckles turned white as she held tightly to her seatbelt. What did he say? These bouts of fear were happening more and more. The triggers were frequent, and it worried him. If she didn't open up soon about what was going on with her, he'd have no other choice but to pry it out. After what she'd been through over the last month with her memory and dealing with the recent death of her own father, asking her to recall something that obviously upset her wasn't on his how-to-win-the-girl list.

He reached for her hand. Her pulse quickened. She was panicked. What was it? What gave her such a fright? He kept his hand on hers for several seconds, wordlessly willing her to come around.

Calm her, Lord.

She stared out the windows, frantically searching for something or someone until she was sure there was nothing to be found. He felt her squeeze and knew he could release her. She was over it.

Nicholas sighed, praying silently for what he should do. The time was coming when he'd call her out, when he'd sit by her side until she let go of whatever had a hold on her. She left him no choice. If they were to have any kind of future together, they needed to know everything about each other. But that time wasn't now. He'd wait until he felt the gentle push from God.

He reached into the bag and pulled out a french fry. He passed her one.

"Now, Sydney Hallaway, I just may have another first for you." He nodded at the fry still holding it out to her. "Take it."

"I really don't want anything other than a few sips of this shake, Nicholas," she pleaded.

"I'm not asking you to eat a meal, just one fry. Here, like this." He dipped a fry in his milkshake and threw the bite into his mouth.

She grimaced. "That's disgusting."

"Says the girl who eats hot dogs. Just try it. If you don't like it, I'll . . . I'll let you pick the next movie, even if it's a sappy chick flick, and I won't complain," he promised.

Charlotte looked at the fry now in her hand. "Go ahead and plan on a couple of hours of the sappiest I can find." She dropped it into her peach shake and hesitantly took a bite. Her facial expression relaxed. "Well," she slowly conceded, "I guess another gun-blazing and mass-destruction movie is on the menu."

Nicholas lifted his head in laughter. "I told you. You should trust me. Sweet and salty are the best. Didn't we agree on that the first day we met?"

She smiled. "I do recall something of that nature." She reached for another fry. "I'll try to remember you're to be trusted, at least with anything sweet and salty."

"Thank you. Appreciated." He looked at her, feeling helpless. He wanted to help with whatever was going on, but he didn't know how. He could mend a fence or figure out a wiring problem, but Charlotte's problem remained a mystery. How could he fix something if he didn't know what was broken? She'd told him everything about herself; he felt sure of it. *Everything, that is, but the root of her fear episodes.*

"Nicholas?"

"Mm?" Pink liquid dripped from his chin. He grabbed a napkin off his lap and dabbed it.

"Thank you for staying with me today. I can't explain it, but I felt safe with you there."

He looked over at her, seeing into her deep brown eyes. "Syd, you know you're always safe with me, right?" He hoped she'd read between the lines. He'd do what he could to keep her safe physically, but would also do what he could to protect her thoughts, her emotions, her past. Her mental well-being was just as important to him. He'd do everything in his power to see her through this pool of uncertainty, if God allowed.

"Yes, I know."

8:15 p.m.

The parking lot was well lit, showing its fairly empty status. Most of the extended-stay guests, who weren't many to begin with, were still out, enjoying what little Jennings had to offer. Nicholas and Charlotte walked into the hotel lobby. The clerk at the front desk saw them and silently motioned them over.

"Someone dropped this off for you," the older gentleman said as he slid an envelope in Charlotte's direction.

Her heart stopped. She stared at it, unsure if she should open it.

Nicholas glanced at her name. "That looks like Vin's handwriting," he said curiously.

Charlotte studied the lettering. It did. She quickly peeled it open.

Don't go back to your room. He knows. I'm in the next room, Room 133. If Nick's still with you, bring him.

Nicholas skimmed the note over her shoulder.

"What's he talking about, Sydney?"

Charlotte tensed. Zeke must've recognized her. But even if he did, how would he know where to find her? Why couldn't she go back to her own room? She hadn't signed her real name for the package.

"Thank you," she offered to the desk clerk as she grabbed Nicholas' hand. She shuffled him briskly in the direction of Room 133 without saying a word.

Her touch held like a death grip, and Nicholas couldn't shake the feeling that his Friday night was just beginning. They found the room near the end of the hall, close to the back exit. Charlotte gently knocked on the door. It opened swiftly.

"Oh, thank You, God!" Vincent hurriedly pulled them in and bolted the lock.

"Vin?" Nicholas asked, staring at his best friend in utter confusion. "What's going on?"

Vincent walked to the chair against the outer wall. Sweat dripped from his sandy hair. He gestured toward the bed and extra chair. "We should be fine here to wait it out. This room and several rooms on either side of us were rented indefinitely the day Charlotte moved in, just in case. But I'm hoping it doesn't matter. They're supposed to call us when this whole thing is over."

"In case what?" Nicholas replied.

"How?" asked Charlotte. "I didn't think he recognized me. And I purposely didn't write the names Charlotte or Sydney."

"I know. And that was brilliant, truly brilliant. I figured out your message as soon as Zeke called."

Nicholas stood, a little frustrated. "Okay, I don't mean to interrupt this little thing you seem to have going with my girlfriend, but maybe you need to start talking."

Charlotte hadn't seen this side of him before. He almost sounded aggressive . . . and a bit possessive. He'd called her *girlfriend*. She doubted she'd ever tire of hearing that.

She looked to Vincent, begging him. "Please, I need him to know."

He nodded. "I know. It's time." He ran his hands across his thighs, wiping sweat from his palms. "Sit, Nick. You're gonna want to."

Nicholas sat on the edge of the bed next to Charlotte. She grabbed his hand. This would sting.

Vincent began, slowly. "I've been mixed up with some people—the wrong kind of people—and I've done some things I'm not very proud of. Under other circumstances, they'd land me in jail." He looked over at Charlotte. "We can't go anywhere, and there's nothing to do but wait. Why don't you tell your side of it first? It'll make more sense if he hears your involvement from your point of view."

Nicholas pulled his hand out of Charlotte's. What was going on? Why did she know something about his best friend that he didn't? What involvement?

Lord, what's going on?

Charlotte's stomach knotted with the withdrawal of his hand. "Okay," she said, silently praying for the words to come out smooth and comprehensible. She kept her eyes on the ground as she spoke, afraid to see his reaction. "I told you I'd taken a bus trip after my father passed, right? And that the bus crashed, and I hit my head, causing my memory loss?"

She sensed his silent nod. "Well, there's a little more to it than that." She hesitated, breathing in the courage she needed. She knew she was only following orders from Detective Jones, but the fact that those orders meant she had to keep quiet and not tell the one man she wanted to tell, made her heart break. She hoped he'd forgive her.

"Yes, it crashed, and yes, I hit my head. But the reason I ended up in those woods wasn't because I'd gotten lost and was walking aimlessly. I crawled out of the wrecked bus and ran because I was afraid. I was afraid I was being chased."

"Chased? By whom?" Was this the reason Charlotte had those horrible bouts with fear? The blood rushed through his veins as he thought about someone hunting her.

"After Dad died, I wanted to get away. I just needed to deal with his death away from home, you know? So I got on a bus to Florida. When we stopped for a quick break about an hour from here, I ran into the store across the terminal to grab some film for my camera. When I did . . ." she glanced at Vincent. He nodded, encouraging her to continue. "I saw Vincent and another guy. They were . . . making an exchange . . . of drugs."

Nicholas shot his friend a look. "What?"

"They spotted me," Charlotte continued, "and changed their minds. They put the drugs back in their book bag. The whole thing shocked me. I just stood there frozen, watching them. An instant later, a teenage boy walked up behind them, but they didn't see him. They didn't know he was there. The man with Vincent swung the bag over his shoulder and hit the worker." Charlotte paused, a quiet tear sliding down her cheek.

Vincent saw her expression and interceded. "The bag knocked him down, and he hit his head on the corner of the counter." He exhaled deeply. "We killed him, Nick. We killed the kid, and Charlotte saw the whole thing."

Nicholas was speechless. What did they just say? It took several seconds for the words to register. His eyes filled with heart-wrenching sadness and then undeniable anger. He stood, clinching his fists shut. He began pacing the small room as muscles flexed in his forearms.

"Seriously, Vin?" he growled slowly while swinging around, ready to take his emotion out on the man he thought he knew. "What were you thinking? How could you? How could you get involved with people like that? How could you be mixed up with drugs and then . . . and then manslaughter? Who are you, man?" he probed angrily. "What kind of man would do such a thing? And Sydney!" He threw his arm in her direction. "*You* did this to her! *You* are the reason she lost her memory and is scared to death half the time."

He glared at Vincent. Fury welled up inside, ready to explode. "She got her memory back a week-and-a-half ago, when she was with you!" The thought made him sick. "What did you do to her? What did you say? Did you threaten her?" He walked over to Vincent, standing within inches of his face. "Vincent, I swear, if you did or said anything to hurt her—"

Charlotte strolled over to Nicholas, gently sliding her hand into his. His chest heaved up and down as she heard his teeth grind. She pulled him back to the edge of the bed.

"Nicholas," she said calmly. "Look at me. Look at me a minute."

He turned to face her. She smiled with content. Fear wasn't in her expression at the moment. "I'm fine. Vincent did not hurt me—ever." She glanced over at the man sitting in the chair, anguish all over his face. "He's been protecting me," she sighed.

"The morning after your dad had his heart attack, he came over to Nellie's with the intentions of telling me everything. When he did, the sight of the book bag over his partner's shoulder came back to me. It all came back. I remembered everything." She cleared her throat. "I was petrified and yelled at him to leave me alone. Of course he did, but not before encouraging me to call the police."

Nicholas scowled at the stranger in the room. He kept his eyes locked on him as he spoke. "Did you?"

"Yes," Charlotte continued, "I did. I talked to a Detective Jones. He told me he knew everything, even about the kid's death." Nicholas lifted his gaze from Vincent and set it on Charlotte. "He told me I could be put under protective custody, or I could help them nail their boss while they watched me from afar. But I wasn't allowed to talk to anyone, other than Vincent, about it." She pleaded with him. "I'm so sorry I lied to you, Nicholas. I wanted so much to tell you."

Nicholas shook his head, trying to put all the pieces together. He looked back at Vincent. "I don't understand. If the cops already knew everything, why didn't they arrest you?"

"I've been an informant for the last year. I couldn't just let her go, man. Not after he died, and I found out."

"That makes no sense, Vincent!"

"I know, Nick, but just hear me out. Please." Vincent ran his hands through his hair. "There's more—parts that Charlotte doesn't even know yet."

Charlotte looked up, confused. She thought she knew everything. What else could there be?

"It's about Nellie," Vincent exhaled. "Yes, I love her—always have—but it's more than that. I had to do everything I could to make sure she was safe. The man she married, the man who is the father of her child and your brother-in-law, wasn't as forthcoming as we all imagined. It's true, he was good to Nellie, and they had a wonderful marriage; but as soon as his brother tried to pull him into the business, things went south."

"Ken has more than one brother?" asked Charlotte and Nicholas simultaneously.

"No." Vincent let that thought linger as the realization of a suddenly mysterious Andy registered with both of them. "Andy Yates also goes by Roland."

Charlotte's eyes widened. *Andy* was the big fish?

"Ken knew his brother played on the wrong side of the law, but chose not to mention that fact to anyone. Instead, he moved from his hometown, met Nellie, and pretended that nothing was wrong. Roland had left him alone for years until a few months after he and Nellie were married. I guess that's when he decided it needed to be a family business. He tried convincing Ken to join him in one or all of his illegal endeavors. Ken, of course, told him to get lost, that he had a wife to take care of, that he had a happy life and wanted nothing to do with any of it."

Vincent rubbed the back of his neck. A year's worth of tension had built up quite a knot. "Roland said he understood and agreed to leave Ken alone. But Ken knew his brother. He knew his tone of voice when he lied. He knew his secret, malicious behavior when things didn't go his way.

"So, believe it or not, he turned to me. I was supposed to be a backup plan, just in case. Ken came to me the day after Roland approached him and explained the whole thing. He said he already knew how much I loved his wife and knew I'd do what I could to protect her if needed. Honestly, I think he had a gut feeling that he wouldn't be around to protect her himself."

"What are you saying?" questioned Nicholas in disbelief. "Andy somehow killed his own brother? Because Ken didn't go along with his schemes?"

"That's exactly what I'm saying. There were no witnesses, and there was no evidence; but I'm convinced Roland killed Ken. It's just too coincidental. It wasn't three days after Ken talked to me that he was dead."

Nicholas interlocked his hands behind his head and looked at the ceiling, trying to make sense of what he was hearing.

"Andy, a.k.a Roland Yates, is dangerous and conniving, controlling crimes from behind the curtain. Just in the drug game alone, he's headed up multiple high-dollar, high-profile drug exchanges and threatened in more ways than one. We're pretty sure he'll dispose of those who get in between him and his agenda. His threats aren't bluffs; he's serious." Vincent's hand shook with the admittance of all he knew. "I had to—needed to—make sure Nellie was okay."

Charlotte let out the gasp she'd been holding. She felt like she could vomit. They'd been under the same roof, had conversations.

She'd interacted with him and been alone in the same room with him, no one around except a helpless baby. All this time, she'd viewed his behavior as a bored or cautious lady's man. How could she have missed it? How could she have not seen behind that flat tone of his? Those crazy eyes? And what about Nellie? Nellie was innocent in all this. What did that mean for her safety and for Walker's? They were his family. They interacted with him day after day.

Nicholas stood abruptly, knocking a throw pillow off the bed with his sudden movement. His voice cracked with tense anger.

"Are you telling me . . . that my *sister* could be with a man right now, a man that may or may not think twice about *killing* someone?" He was on the brink of losing any cool he had left.

Vincent rose from his chair, coming face-to-face with his friend. "Yes," he said slowly, "but the police have been watching her, and now Walker, since the beginning. I swear, Nick."

"If you knew what kind of man he was, why on earth did you not tell Nellie?" Pure rage tainted his voice.

"The day Ken died, I went to the police. I told them everything Ken had told me. I admitted my suspicions about his death and my concerns for Nellie. They explained they had nothing to show for it. Said the accident looked like it was just that—an accident. It was all just hearsay. There wasn't anything they could do at the moment other than keep an eye out, and they advised me not to mention what I suspected to Nellie. They thought her knowing would put her in danger because she wouldn't be herself around Roland. He'd get suspicious. Plus, her husband had just died, and she was in no shape to deal with the possibility that his death was intentional. So, I kept my mouth shut and watched her like a hawk.

"At the funeral and the days that followed, Roland observed me. He saw that I was overly committed to his brother's wife. He thought he could use that to his advantage. He misinterpreted my commitment to her. Thought I had some boyhood crush. Never realized I actually loved her and was there to protect her. He had no idea that I was on to him."

Nicholas started to pace. His fists pumped open and closed as he listened to the nightmare coming to life before him.

"Almost two months after Ken's death and six weeks after Nellie realized she was pregnant, Roland said he wanted me to meet someone. He thought he could use my past and present actions toward your sister against me. He was trying to decide if I could be persuaded into becoming one of his suppliers, since I have access to one of his drugs of choice at the clinic.

"He thought if he could get me to do something illegal just one time, he'd have me. I'd be framed, and Nellie would never trust me again if she found out. I was a perfect fit for his little ring of criminals. What better way to make someone loyal than by manipulating him into obedience?"

He paused, sticking his still-shaking hands into his pockets. "Roland told me someone was interested in becoming a vet. Said the guy was trying to decide if he and vet school were a good fit and wanted to talk about some career shadowing. I agreed and met the guy, Zeke, at some store where he supposedly worked, during what was supposed to be his lunch break. When I got there, things happened; and before I knew it, I'd been framed for theft." Vincent rolled his eyes at his own stupidity.

"Zeke quickly told me we were both on the store's surveillance footage. He said Roland would have the tape." He sighed heavily. "I didn't steal anything, but it was made very clear that it looked like I did. They had proof, no matter how fake it was. Roland essentially blackmailed me. Said he'd show the tape to Nellie and to the cops if I didn't join him."

Vincent finally sat back down, followed by Nicholas, hesitantly.

"What Roland didn't count on was my going to the police. I went to them that same night and explained everything, hoping they'd believe me. I knew if I waited another day, to dwell on it any longer than necessary, the look of my innocence diminished greatly. It was kind of an all-or-nothing shot in the dark.

"I met Detective Jones and explained the whole thing. He pulled the reported suspicion I'd filed not long before and put events together in his head, saying there'd been a string of drug disappearances at medical facilities and a couple missing persons within a four-hour drive from Jennings in all directions. He felt they could all be possibly connected somehow, but he couldn't be sure. At the same time, he didn't want to make the mistake of assuming they weren't. He didn't have much of a lead, until I gave him the two names—Zeke Morrison and Roland/Andy Yates. It was the first positive thing he had to work with."

Vincent reached in the small refrigerator and pulled out a bottle of water. He silently asked if the others wanted one. They refused. He took a sip, cooling his throat.

"They needed solid evidence that Roland and Zeke were behind the other suspected crimes. Jones offered me the job of informant. I accepted on one condition—that Nellie be protected." He half-smiled to himself. "If she knew how they took that literally, how much her privacy is being invaded, she'd never acknowledge me again." He put the water on the ground.

"Nothing?" Nicholas interrupted. "They've really got nothing on this guy? No recorded calls or anything?"

"My phones—all my phones—work, home, cell—are tapped, just in case. Unfortunately, Roland uses a burner when he's making business calls to Zeke. And he never calls me, unless it's for casual talk. If he has information that needs to get to us quickly, he calls Zeke, and then Zeke passes the message to me. He's smart. All other times, the instructions for an exchange are written, and there's no way to trace the letters back to him. I'm telling you, he's smart, too smart."

Vincent peered over at Charlotte, who sat with her mouth open, trying to digest everything he'd just said. It was a lot to take in at once. He wanted to tell her earlier, to prepare her, but the police were afraid she wouldn't be able to act normal around Nellie. And that would draw suspicion. It was bad enough she had to act like nothing happened around him. He clenched his teeth, wishing she'd taken the way out two weeks ago.

"I had Zeke tell me everything he told Roland after he left Uncle Bob's store. You did a great job with the name, Charlotte. I'm impressed you were able to think that through under that kind of pressure. But," he hesitated. "He also gave him a description of you, saying you were kind of short, wore glasses, have brown hair, and lots of freckles."

"Oh," Charlotte said, finally seeing the reason for the room.

"Yeah, Roland knows Charlotte, the girl who showed up to town without a memory. He knows you wear glasses and have freckles. They're kind of hard to miss. And most importantly, he knows your memory returned, and therefore, you had to have recognized me. Roland, no doubt, has just put all the pieces together and is on his way over here as we speak."

Charlotte's shoulders shuddered. "What about Detective Jones?"

"As soon as Zeke called to tell me he'd spotted you, I made sure he wasn't following you, and then I called Detective Jones. He said he'd just gotten off the phone with you." Nicholas looked at Charlotte, trying to figure out when she had time to make that call. "He suggested I get here as fast as I could. He also told me Nick was with you and that he'd have a man on you and a man on Nellie. Supposedly she's at home, alone at the moment, with Walker."

"And Andy? Where is he?" asked Nicholas.

"We don't know. They lost him not too long after four. My guess is that he disappeared pretty soon after Zeke called him and he figured it all out. I told you, he's smart. I really think he knew my phones were bugged and that he'd been under suspicion. He goes off grid every once in a while, probably when he's deciding on a target or wrapping up some loose ends, and then shows up again, cool and collected, living the life of a responsible salesman as he helps out his deceased brother's wife and child."

Charlotte couldn't speak. She couldn't wrap her head around the cold and calculated operation this man had instigated, the time he put into it. Nicholas asked the question she herself suddenly pondered. "So, Nellie, their relationship? That was just a cover?"

Vincent's face grimaced in pain. It hurt him to say because he wanted so much for Nellie to be happy, to be loved by all the way he knew she should be loved.

"Yes." Nicholas dropped his head into his hands. "I'm pretty sure his relationship with her is a fake, a protective means to an end, and a way to get close to his nephew. I honestly do think he cares for

Walker. He's blood, a part of his brother, but I'm betting he could care less for Nellie."

Vincent sighed. "Truth is, I believe he'd probably skip town if it wasn't for the baby. The only way to be cleared and possibly make Walker his is to finish things here. That means getting rid of anyone who could connect him to a crime. Right now, that leaves us. He knows that Charlotte can identify me, and he now knows I'm likely working with the police." He stopped, thinking about the possible outcome. "My bet is he gets rid of Zeke, too, by pinning our disappearances on him."

Charlotte's hands trembled. She and Nicholas had sat patiently, listening to Vincent Cobb tell a tale of unheard-of proportions. He recounted the information with sheer determination and speed, as if he needed to get everything out in the open before her world ended, before his world ended.

The room spun, blurring the two men with her together, forming one individual. She felt sick. The headache she'd been free of since her first days in Jennings, Georgia, resurfaced, greater in its intensity.

What was she going to do? Her life was in the hands of so many others, of Detective Jones and the police, of Vincent and Nicholas, and of Andy Yates. She felt the blood drain from her face as she all but fell to the stained carpet between the bed and the bathroom wall.

Oh, God. I'm so scared. I'm so confused.

Vincent and Nicholas continued talking, unaware of her thoughts. She struggled to breathe. Flashes of her brother, her mother, and her father, all in their coffins, lifeless and with arms folded across their chests, filled her mind. Was her entire family destined to die young? Was there no hope for any of the Hallaways? She wanted to cry, but the tears wouldn't come.

A soft thought pulled at her heart. In the midst of the heated chatter between Vincent and Nicholas and the air conditioner kicking in by the window and the screams of confusion within her mind, Charlotte heard a gentle whisper. She closed her eyes and let it cover her like a blanket.

Your life is Mine.

Her shallow breathing steadied. Her racing heartbeat slowed. She tilted her head back against the wall and surrendered her fears to the One who truly did hold her life in His hands—Who created her, Who loved her, Who knew even the number of hairs on her head and the days she was blessed to live.

If You're calling me Home, God, help me to accept it. If not, help me to be strong enough to get through this. Give me wisdom. Help me to fear no evil, for You are with me, God. You are my Shield, oh, Lord. Be that for all of us. Open my eyes so that I can see clearly through all the confusion, all the chaos. Somehow, be glorified, be just.

9:05 p.m.

They heard a knock at the door. The room went silent. Nicholas pointed to the bed. Charlotte slid underneath, hugging the headboard wall. Vincent unplugged the lamp on the small, round table by the window, wrapping its chord around the base. Nicholas did the same with the bedside lamp.

Vincent peeked through the peephole. It was Nellie. He gasped as he saw the barrel of a gun pressed against her temple. Vincent swung around, terror in his eyes. He mouthed the words, "It's Nellie—at gunpoint!"

Nicholas shook with anger. Tremors moved down his body. How did that happen? How had Roland gotten her without the cops knowing? And how had he gotten into this building unnoticed? An officer was supposed to be watching over Charlotte. Vincent peered through the hole again. The gun had been lowered to what he assumed, was her back, under the jacket spread over his arm.

Nellie was terrified. Tears streamed down her face. She looked lost, trying to understand what was happening. Vincent pulled out his cell phone and swiftly sent a text to Detective Jones. Roland knocked again.

"Vinnie, I think we need to have a talk." His tone was calm, menacing. "The little set-up we had is over. Time to let me in. I'd like to see that annoying other uncle, too. Oh, and of course, we can't forget the 'belle of the ball'—the reason we're all here in the first place."

Nicholas tightened his grip around the lamp. He could hear his sister sniffling through the door and his girlfriend gasping under the bed. Vincent's phone vibrated in his pocket. He quickly checked it and hurried to unlock the window with the security code Jones sent. The small-town, extended-stay had recently installed new windows that operated much like a coded safe. Each resident was issued keys to their door and a code to their window. It was an added security feature, but it was still in the testing phase. Tonight, they'd be put to the ultimate test. The cavalry was on its way. If they could hold Roland off for a few more minutes, help would arrive.

Vincent thought about sending Charlotte through the window, getting her as far from any threat as he could. But he didn't know where Zeke was at the moment. He could be hiding in the parking lot or somewhere inside the building. If Roland got past Charlotte's assigned detail, there was a dangerous reason. She may be safer with them inside this room.

He looked over at Nicholas speaking to him with his eyes, the way they'd always done in the woods, hunting for game. Nicholas understood and stepped between the bed and the wall, forming a boundary between Charlotte and the unknown. He eyed the window, praying Roland wouldn't notice the blinking red light, indicating it was unlocked.

Vincent turned his attention back to Roland. If they didn't let him in, unsuspecting residents could be caught in a crossfire. He slowly lifted the chain out of its socket and opened the door. Roland thrust his sister-in-law over the threshold, a 9 mm pistol pressed against her back with one hand and covering her mouth with the other. Vincent growled. Nicholas ground his teeth, his jaw tightening.

"It wasn't Charlotte's fault, Roland. She's an innocent," baited Vincent.

Roland laughed. "An innocent? Come on, Vinnie. No one's innocent when they witness something on my watch. You should know that better than anyone. You've heard the stories."

Nellie let out a scream, muffled by her kidnapper's hands. Her eyes widened in sheer terror. Roland shoved her into a chair and told her to be quiet, keeping the gun directly at her head.

"Where's Walker?" asked Nicholas, between clenched teeth.

"Oh, he's fine. Don't you worry, Uncle Nick. My sister has him at Nellie's place. She was more than happy to watch him, while I took the little sis-in-law here out to dinner." He waved the gun in the air as a quick reminder of his control of the situation. "Nellie was all too willing to have a knight in shining armor mysteriously whisk her away from a tiring day of playing mom. She thought the trek through the back woods was an adventure, didn't you, sis?"

Nellie tried to stand, to get away. Roland plunged her back down, causing immediate pain in her left shoulder.

"Still haven't figured out what my brother saw in you. You're nothing but a goody-two-shoes—utterly boring and barely above-average looking," he said. Vincent's fist balled as Roland let out a menacing laugh. "Calm down, Vinnie. I said above-average." He stroked her hair with the gun's barrel.

"Nellie loves it when I surprise her with a good picnic. I do stuff like that quite often, you know. After all, I can be my brother when I want to be. It couldn't have been easier to disappear from those men you had following her."

A shiver traveled slowly down Charlotte's back, reaching every nerve she had. She couldn't see what was going on, but she could hear it. Roland Yates sounded ruthless. He no longer sounded like the flat businessman who wanted only to flirt with his eyes. Now he sounded evil.

"Okay," Roland said calmly, "I'm going to need you boys to put the lamps down, pull the girl out from wherever she's hiding, and then we're all going to walk out of here like we're having the time of our lives. I'm thinking a drive would do us all some good. How about you?" He pushed the barrel into Nellie's head, stressing his command for obedience.

They had no other choice. If they didn't go with him, he could kill Nellie right in front of them. The men glanced at each other, simultaneously putting down the lamps. Nicholas reached his hand under the bed, grabbing Charlotte, and helped her out. She looked at him in desperation, hoping he could read her heart, all of it—the fear she had at the moment and the love she had for the grizzly man from the woods. She may never get the chance to tell him how she felt.

From somewhere deep, Nicholas found the strength to smile at Charlotte. She slowly lowered her eyes and nodded, knowing he knew.

Vincent walked past Nellie as he headed to the door. He gently squeezed her elbow, trying to reassure her. Nicholas glanced at the window one last time, silently praying. He took Charlotte's hand and followed Vincent out the door, into the hallway.

As soon as they turned the corner of Room 133's doorframe, Vincent, Nicholas, and Charlotte were jerked into the adjacent room. Charlotte's body hadn't cleared before Roland exited the room with Nellie, catching the attempted escape. He pushed Nellie to the side and reached for Charlotte, grasping her arm. Nellie fell to the ground. Men rushed out of the empty rooms that had been rented. Roland, still holding tightly to Charlotte, lurched her back into Room 133. He slammed the door and turned around. Three officers with pointed guns stood just inside the window. He glanced at the blinking red light, noticing it too late.

Roland pulled Charlotte close, holding her arm tight enough to bruise it.

"It's over, Roland. Put your weapon down."

"Nothing's over. I've worked too hard and too long to give up now."

He aimed his gun at Charlotte's head as he walked slowly toward the officers. They kept their weapons raised, but moved to the side, careful to give him enough space. They wouldn't risk a civilian's life. Within seconds, they'd all switched places. Roland and Charlotte were close enough to the open window to feel the night's breeze.

There was hardly enough time for Charlotte to adjust being thrown into Nellie's position of hostage before Roland pulled her through the window, using her as a shield between himself and the men. She was his ticket out of there.

Charlotte's foot caught on the ledge on her way out. She fell to the pavement next to him. The fall loosened his grip on her arm and knocked the gun from his hand. Pain shot through her right knee. She ignored it. She did not think. She did not hesitate. She quickly jerked out of his slackened hold and jumped from his outreached hand. She ran, sprinting through the back parking lot as fast as she could.

She didn't know if Zeke was there waiting for her, if Roland was right behind her, or if she was free. She just ran. She ran clear across the parking lot and the empty acre behind the building before she heard two gunshots. A ripping pain glided across her upper arm. Her legs jolted to a stop.

Charlotte slowly turned, her uninjured arm raised in defeat. She couldn't outrun a bullet. As she descended to the ground, suddenly too weak to stand, her mouth dropped at the sight in front of her. Roland Yates lay thirty feet from her, face down—dead. Smoke from the gun still in his right hand rose from the barrel.

CHAPTER TEN

Saturday, April 23

1:45 a.m.

"Okay, I think we've got it. You're free to go, Ms. Hallaway, and thank you for your cooperation." The officer taking her statement opened the door, dismissing her. Nicholas Nelson stood at the sight of Charlotte. She tried walking forward, but her feet refused to move. He rushed to her side and wrapped his arm around her back. She was safe, once again, in the arms of her hunter. He gently and slowly guided her out of the Jennings Police Department and into his truck.

He turned on the vehicle and drove to his house, where Nellie and Walker were waiting with Vincent. She remained quiet as she stared out the window. There was a full moon. Houses and trees could still be seen at close range, even though it was far past midnight. Nicholas pulled into his driveway and slid the gear into PARK.

He slipped off his seatbelt and moved next to Charlotte. She leaned into his embrace and cried. She let out all the fear she'd felt over the last two weeks. She released the uncertainties and confusions, the loss of her family's life and the safety of her own. God had spared them all, even the officer assigned to watch Charlotte. He thankfully only suffered the humiliation of distraction. God brought everyone away unharmed, except for the insignificant scratch on Charlotte's right arm. The bullet Roland had fired had grazed her, requiring four stitches. She'd never been more grateful for stitches in her life.

Nicholas let Charlotte cry until he felt her begin to shudder. It was the point his sister always got to when she tried to calm herself down.

"You're safe now, Sydney. No one will hurt you again, not on my watch."

She lifted her head and reached for the extra napkins she knew he kept in the glove compartment. She blew her nose.

"What about Zeke? He's still out there."

He smiled. "No, actually he's not. The cops picked him up at his house. Now that Andy is out of the picture, they don't need him to be the dummy runner, so to speak. They've taken him in. They already had enough evidence to convict Zeke. It'd been Andy they needed evidence for. He was the main one they wanted. That's why they needed Vin as an informant." He reached over and pulled out another napkin, handing it to her. She blew again.

"He's clearly not quite as smart as Andy. Vin thought he'd probably go home to collect his own personal stockpile—one Andy knew nothing about. Turns out, Zeke had tucked away a small portion of the drugs with every exchange he'd made over the years, grabbing what he thought he could get away with. Vincent knew about it and told the police. They found the stash under his mattress in his bedroom."

"So, he's in jail?" she asked, hope filling her voice.

He pulled her close. "Yes, Syd, he's in jail. And he's not getting out anytime soon. Vincent will make sure of that with his testimony."

She exhaled, shaking as the breath escaped. "It's over? All of it? It's really over?"

Nicholas bent down, kissing her gently on the top of her head. "Yes, my dear. It's over, every bit of it."

Oh, thank You, Lord!

They sat in silence for several minutes, each praising God for the night's end. He had delivered them. He'd put an end to Charlotte's nightmares. She was free—free from carrying the burden of what she'd witnessed and free from the secrets she'd been forced to keep. Renewed strength washed over her.

"Nicholas," she said, lifting her head from his chest, "can you forgive me?"

Confused, he looked at her. "For what? All of this has been done *to* you, not *because* of you."

Her plea was genuine. "For lying to you by omission." She sat up straight. "I didn't tell you about Vincent. I didn't tell you about any of it."

"Of course," he said, slipping his hand into hers. "You were following orders, and I understand that. I just hate you had to go through all of it alone."

"I wasn't alone, not after I learned to trust Vincent. He was actually a big help. He called and came by a lot. It bothered him, I mean really bothered him, that his decision to help the police had put me in danger. It truly upset him that I'd lost my memory. After that poor boy was accidently killed, he wanted out. Roland was the suspected one behind people disappearing. But the kid at the store was the first one that Vincent had ever been a part of.

"He told me he regretted getting involved in the first place. Said he should've trusted God to handle it His way, but he was in too deep. As much as he wanted to, they'd all put too much into his cover for him to pull out at the last minute." She felt Nicholas' thumb rubbing over the back of her hand.

"That was why he came to me that morning, the day after your dad was put in the hospital. Vincent wanted to trigger my memory. He wanted it to scare me enough that I'd go to the police. He'd hoped my memory returning would be the end to it. He assumed I'd tell everyone."

"But you didn't. Why?"

"I saw the anguish, the forgiveness he sought. I saw it in his face, his up-and-down emotions, and in the ways he tried to get me to reveal his true identity. I also understood the reason we were both asked to help bring down Andy, though I didn't know it was Andy at the time."

Nicholas dropped his head against the headrest. "I guess I owe Vin an apology. I doubted his character, one I've known our whole lives, and was ready to pummel him."

Charlotte laughed. "Yes, you were. I have now seen the Hulk side of you."

"I guess you have, haven't you? Sorry about that. I'll try to keep the green away from now on."

She smiled, proud of the humility he possessed. A man admitting a wrong—another quality she liked.

"So, does your mom know?" she asked, feeling more like herself the longer they talked.

"Not yet. She's away for the weekend, at a conference with a friend. We want to get it all worked out in our own heads before we tell her. She doesn't need another emotional situation to deal with right now. We'll call her tomorrow and let her know, when we are hopefully all calm enough to talk about it." He stretched his legs to the side.

"How about Andy's sister? What's going on with her?"

"The police are taking her in for questioning. I don't think she had any knowledge of her brother's crimes, though. She seemed genuinely shocked and very upset when they picked up Walker to give to Nellie. She didn't seem to have any idea of what was going on in her own family, and now two brothers are dead. It's going to be a pretty rough road of healing ahead for her."

Charlotte sighed. "Nellie's will be, too."

Nicholas closed his eyes in pain for his sister. Charlotte was right. It'd take some time for Nellie to get past this. She never saw it coming. Her husband—murdered by his own brother. Though it wasn't a long marriage, it was a good one. Ken's death was so abrupt and pointless.

It'd take quite a while to come to terms with the sudden change in her life, but Nicholas knew she wouldn't go through it alone. Nellie had her relationship with God, her family, Charlotte, and quite loyally, Vincent Cobb. She'd see eventually that his love for her was deep, that he did what he did for her. He'd wait for Nellie for as long as he needed to, standing solidly by her side, protecting and helping her.

Nicholas reached for the door. "Ready to go in?"

"Yes. I'm ready."

CHAPTER ELEVEN

Saturday, October 15

Nicholas Nelson paced the driveway. Charlotte had been away from Jennings for six months, not counting the handful of long weekend visits. She wanted to complete one more semester of graduate school back home before transferring to an online program through the University of Georgia. The online option allowed her to move permanently to Jennings. After stretching her schooling out over several years so she could take care of her father after his first stroke, Charlotte was on track to actually finish. In another five months, she'd finally have her MBA. With her impending diploma, the Cranes had asked her to run their shop. Since their son, Jeff, didn't want it, choosing instead a life in the big city of Dallas, Texas, Charlotte happily agreed.

When those long weekends came around, Nicholas and Charlotte spent almost every bit of that time together. They rode horses; took walks; hung out with Vincent, Nellie, and Walker; and watched movies. They even took a day trip to the beach with Mrs. Nelson, hoping to ease some of her loneliness. She'd decided to move back home, insisting it was time she dealt with her own life's sorrows. She'd focused all her attention on filling her days without down-time, trying to run away from the pain. But after a heart-to-heart conversation with her son, she knew she couldn't continue her life that way. She needed to face reality.

Patricia Nelson heard Charlotte's story and was amazed with her ability to handle what she'd been through. She was so captivated by Charlotte's kindheartedness and her strength that she listened intently to Charlotte as she explained how she survived, from beginning to end. She heard the source of that strength, coming to finally see the Truth for herself. Once she accepted Christ, her loneliness wasn't as empty. She still grieved, but she now felt the arms of her Savior while she cried. She felt His comfort and His promise of a sunrise each day.

With the lift in her spirits and the motivation of her God, Mrs. Nelson faced her world of meetings and fashion and politics as a new woman. She now used her platform in the community to speak about Jesus, reaching dozens of ladies who'd normally turn a deaf ear. But because the words came from one of their own, they listened. They heard. They accepted. And they, themselves, shared the newfound knowledge with others.

"There she is," Nicholas said, beaming from the excitement. "I've got to go. Call you tonight."

"Tell her I said *welcome home*. And I want to hear everything. Everything, Nick!"

"Okay, okay. Bye, Nellie."

He put the phone in his pocket as Charlotte Hallaway pulled into the driveway of her new home. With the sale of her father's place, she was able to purchase a small, one-story brick house three blocks away from the center of town. Most places were within walking distance, which would be a nice mode of transportation on a cool, autumn day.

The house sat in a quiet neighborhood surrounded by mostly older couples. Trees shaded the roads, making it a perfect atmosphere for her daily run. There wasn't much of a yard, only about a quarter of an acre, but it was hers. She no longer had to bounce back and forth from her old life to her new life, going to school in one place and leaving her heart in another. She could now bring her old life to Jennings, Georgia, where she belonged.

Charlotte stepped out of the U-Haul and stretched her arms. "Well, hey there, favorite person in Jennings."

Nicholas wrapped her in a welcome-home embrace, lifting her off the ground.

"Oh, is it good to see you," he said as he gently placed her back on her feet. "How was your trip? Any trouble driving that big ole thing?"

She smiled, keeping her fingers locked around his neck. "Nah, not too bad. I did decide to go the long way, though. I was afraid those back roads might be too tight for me to handle, since I was pulling my car behind it. I much prefer a four-lane highway to a two."

She released him and walked around to the back of the truck, where she lifted the sliding door. Nicholas grunted, teasingly. "I told you I'd do it for you."

"I know," she grinned. "But I wanted to do it on my own. It felt good, having to hire movers and sell Dad's house. I've been so dependent on others lately. I just wanted to close that chapter all by myself."

He tapped the side of the truck. "Well, my sweet girl, you did. And it looks like you did a great job."

She took an exaggerated bow. "Thank you."

"So," he said, pulling out the packed suitcase at the edge. Charlotte had put what she'd need for a few days in one spot. There was no telling how long it'd take to unpack her life and properly move into her new house. "Nellie has already invited us over for supper. She says she's having pork chops. You interested?"

"Of course," Charlotte almost squealed. She was so ready to be back in the place she planned to call home for years to come. "How is Nellie? I talk to her almost as much as I talk to you, but I can't tell if she's faking it or if she really is doing okay."

"She really is okay. Nights are hardest on her. That's when her mind slows down enough for her to wonder how and why. But then she gets up in the mornings, thankful for Walker and for a new day. I don't expect things to be right as rain for quite a while, but she's getting there."

Charlotte nodded.

"Oh, and guess what she found stuffed behind a drawer in her guest bedroom."

"What?"

"An envelope with two plane tickets to Jamaica, dated a week after Ken died."

"Are you kidding me?" she asked, almost skipping over syllables. "What's that all about?"

"Nellie thinks they were going to be her birthday gift from Ken. Not sure why he hid them there, but he did."

"You think it was more than a birthday gift? That he hid it there to keep it from Andy's sight during visits? Maybe Ken was trying to protect Nellie and was ready to run."

"Believe it or not," Nicholas answered, "I thought the same thing. But Nellie didn't. She's not even considering Andy. She's holding fast to the idea her husband had another sweet gesture up his sleeve, and I'm not saying a word."

"Smart," Charlotte agreed. "What's she going to do with the tickets? Will they refund them?"

"She explained the situation to the airline, and they've told her she can change the date when she's ready—provided she changes it within a year."

He put the box down to get a better grip and picked it up again.

"Amazing." It made Charlotte smile. This small town and surrounding city loved and took care of their own. She was excited to now be a part of it.

They walked to the carport area. "You want to get what we can off the truck before the skies open up?"

Charlotte looked up. She hadn't noticed the dark gray clouds moving in. "Uh, sure, sounds good. Put what we can under here until it starts to rain. Then we can bring it in the house and set it up. Hopefully, it won't be a blowing rain."

"Okay, but let's stack everything close to the inner wall, just in case," Nicholas suggested.

"Good idea." They returned to the truck for more boxes. "And Vincent? Where does he fit into Nellie's life at the moment?"

He chuckled. "Not much higher than he did before, I'm afraid. But he loves her so much, he'll be patient. He's waited twenty years for her. He'll wait twenty more if he has to."

"What if Nellie marries another?"

"Then Vin will do what he did before. He'll back down. But hopefully, he won't have to turn to a life of crime to protect her again."

"Poor Vincent," said Charlotte, feeling sorry for the man who had once come across as awkward.

Nicholas pulled down a large box labeled *master bathroom and bedroom*. "Don't feel sorry for him. He's as content as I've ever seen him. Nellie is safe, and that was all that mattered to him. Honestly, now that I think about it, he hasn't been this content in over a year-and-a-half, since I guess about the time he found out Ken came with baggage." He shifted his hands on the box. "As long as my sister is safe, there's always a chance she'll be happy again. And if Nellie is safe *and* happy, Vincent will be, too. Of course, he'd like to be the reason for her happiness, but he'll adjust if needed."

After fifteen minutes, a light mist began to fall, causing a halt to the unloading. "Come on, let's head inside. I haven't seen you in quite a while, and I'd like to give my girl a proper hug before we start stinking from all this heavy lifting."

Charlotte put her hands on her hips, contemplating all she wanted to get done before nightfall. She shrugged her shoulders in defeat. "Okay, you win. But only a ten-minute break. Then, if it's still just a mist, we keep at it."

He smiled. "Deal." Nicholas pulled down the U-Haul's back door, and they made their way into the house.

Charlotte walked into her new home, catching a trace of a pine-scented cleaning solvent. Nicholas had obviously cleaned it, getting it ready for her. The lights shone bright from most of the rooms, welcoming her. He'd had the power turned on earlier that week. She stepped through the kitchen. It was set up a lot like Nellie's. She pictured the two of them sitting at the table, drinking coffee and happily discussing something Walker had learned to do. They'd need to come for a visit as soon as she got the house ready. She owed Nellie.

Beyond the kitchen, Charlotte noticed a red and blue quilt spread across the hardwood floor in the den. "What's that? Were you afraid we'd scuff the floor?"

"That should've crossed my mind, but I must admit, it didn't." He reached for a basket behind the pantry door. "Actually," he said, holding the basket in the air, "I was hoping to convince you to take a picnic lunch with me."

Charlotte smiled. "Mmm, so it shouldn't matter that it's two-thirty, and I've already eaten?"

"Nope."

"Well, then, Mr. Nelson, I'd love to share a picnic lunch with you." They sat on the quilt as Nicholas began to unload the basket's contents. "And what did you pack?"

"Let's see," he said in an extreme southern accent. "We've got grilled hot dogs with ketchup and/or mustard, chopped onions, and chili for those of us who need to drown out the taste of the dog, your choice of chips, and a few chocolate kisses for dessert. Oh," he retreated to the kitchen, pulling a pitcher out of the refrigerator he had installed the day before. "And, of course, iced strawberry lemonade to drink."

Charlotte laughed out loud. "You remembered."

"Absolutely. You're important to me." He unwrapped a hot dog from aluminum foil. "Which toppings would you like, Ms. Hallaway?"

She lowered her chin to her chest in pseudo-embarrassment. "I feel bad about saying this, because you've gone to all this trouble, but . . . I eat it plain."

"That's okay. I really brought the rest of it for me. If I'm going to force that thing down, it's going to need help."

She smiled, loving the personality of the man before her. He was everything she'd never dreamt of. When she thought of herself loving someone, she had ideas of who that person would be. She knew he'd love God and would be kind to others, but she'd had no idea how much more he'd exhibit.

Nicholas Nelson was funny. He kept her laughing. He was generous and unselfish, forgiving and humble. He was beyond handsome, making her shudder at times. He was protective, her personal hero. He was so much more than who she could've created for herself if she'd been given the chance. Nicholas was one of God's incredible creations. She planned to relish every minute as his girlfriend.

There were no more barriers, no more bouts of fear or loss of memories, no more misperceptions or doubt. There was only clarity. She'd learned to see clearly through the confusion in her circumstances. She'd learned to trust. She'd learned to let God move where He wanted, using whom He wanted. He'd used a state of chaos in her life and turned it into something beautiful. Charlotte learned God was good, all the time, even in the midst of a storm.

"Before you get your second hot dog," he teased, "I have something for you."

"What makes you think I'm going to eat another?" she asked, curiously.

He chuckled, reaching around the wall beside him. "I saw the way you were eyeing that last one. You're like a lioness, circling her prey with that look of yours."

She threw her arms up in jest. "All right, you've got me. I was eyeing it. You did an excellent job with these. Your grilling is just right," she baited.

"No, no," he laughed, "I will not make you another one tomorrow, at least not for another week. I can't handle them anymore than that."

She grinned and popped her last bite into her mouth. Nicholas pulled out a vase containing one flower. "What's that?" Charlotte asked. "That poor thing looks pitiful."

"She's had better days, true, but she's sacrificing for a purpose."

Charlotte studied the flower Nicholas now had in his hand. He sat on his knees and held it out to her. She looked at it, utter bewilderment filling her mind. He grinned widely as he saw her wheels turning, trying desperately to figure out what was going on.

"Sydney Charlotte Jane Hallaway, you are my sunshine. You encourage me, support me, and trust me. You even call me out when I need it, with gracious understanding and loving forgiveness. You put God first, others second, and yourself third. You are my happy place, and I adore you. I love you, Sydney, so very much. Will you do me the great honor of becoming my wife? Will you marry me?"

Tears filled her eyes. She looked again at the flower he held, suddenly realizing it was the most beautiful flower she'd ever seen. The simple, sweet daisy was the perfect picture of her past, present, and future. Sticking out of its bright yellow center was one white petal—one petal that came with a marriage proposal. He loved her.

I asked one of my daughter's friends, Tatum Ricketson, to draw some inspiration for "Clear Confusion." Thank you Tatum for coming to my rescue. You did a fantabulous job!

Also By Kathy M. Howard:

Bayne Harris has lost everything she holds dear in her life.

Her husband and children are dead. She was the one who caused the accident—the one behind the wheel. She cannot escape that night as it continuously haunts her thoughts.

A year after they're gone, nothing has changed. The memories are still unbearable. She can't breathe. She can't function. She needs to get away.

View Top Mountain provides the perfect escape. No one will bother her there. No one will want to check on her or talk about what happened. She can live her life alone, away from do-gooders and any chance of happiness.

This is her plan, but she soon finds out God has something else in store.

from *Driftwood* to *Sapphire*
a novel

Kathy M. Howard

Samantha Jordan spent her entire life within a family unit of two: herself and her father, Wren—until Bay Harris came into their lives. Now, with the addition of a stepmother, a little sister, and another sister on the way, the family unit has stretched itself to a loving number of five.

She enters her senior year at Brenton College hopeful and happy, planning to make the most of her last year as a student. Although her best friend has graduated, leaving her to a freshman roommate with unusual social problems, Samantha still has Trevor James, a driven and handsome friend from her hometown, View Top Mountain.

However, when tragedy occurs and secrets are revealed, Samantha's world turns upside down and her trust in God is tested.